Christmas in My Heart

16

Joe L. Wheeler

D1614193

REVIEW AND HERALD® PUBLISHING ASSOCIATION

Since 1861 | www.reviewandherald.com

This book was
Edited by Jeannette R. Johnson
Cover illustration by The Old Homestead in Winter, 1864 (litho), by Currier, N. (1813-1888), and Ives, J. M. (1824-1895).
        Kenneth M. Newman / The Old Print Shop, Inc.
Interior illustrations are from the library of Joe L. Wheeler
Typeset: 11/12 Goudy

PRINTED IN U.S.A.
11 10 09 08 07   5 4 3 2 1

R&H Cataloging Service

Wheeler, Joe L., 1936-   , comp.
        Christmas in my heart. Book 16.

        1. Christmas stories, American.   I. Title:
Christmas in my heart. Book 16.

ISBN: 978-0-8280-2029-9

Dedication

In this busy life we lead, it is all too easy to take for granted the ones who do the most for us and mean the most to us. Always, we think there will be plenty of time to thank them later, after we've thanked everyone else first.

Well, I'm not waiting any longer for this one. I'm hereby dedicating *Christmas in My Heart 16* to the one who types out our correspondence, choreographs our e-mails, invoices and packages our book orders, makes our photocopies, answers our phone, helps choose our stories, types out our stories and files them away, makes the edits our editors request . . . and oh the list could go on and on!

Who else could this wonder woman be but my wife and partner in all things:

CONNIE PALMER WHEELER

Books by Joe L. Wheeler

Christmas in My Heart, books 1-16
Christmas in My Heart, audio books 1-6
Easter in My Heart
Everyday Heroes
Great Stories Remembered, I
Great Stories Remembered, II
Great Stories Remembered, III
Great Stories Remembered, audio books I-III
Great Stories Remembered Classic Books (12 books)
Heart to Heart Stories of Dads
Heart to Heart Stories of Moms
Heart to Heart Stories of Friendship
Heart to Heart Stories for Grandparents
Heart to Heart Stories of Love
Heart to Heart Stories for Sisters
Heart to Heart Stories of Teachers
Owney, the Post Office Dog
Remote Controlled
Smokey, the Ugliest Cat in the World
St. Nicholas: A Closer Look at Christmas
Stories of Angels
Time for a Story
What's So Good About Tough Times?
Wings of God, The

Acknowledgments

"Voices From the Past" (Introduction), by Joseph Leininger Wheeler. Copyright © 2006. Printed by permission of the author.

"When the Wise Man Appeared," by William Ashley Anderson. If anyone can provide knowledge of earliest publication source of this old story, or the author's next of kin, please send to Joe Wheeler (P.O. Box 1246, Conifer, CO 80433). Printed with permission of CBS Corporation, Inc.

"Christmas in the Street of Memories," by Elizabeth Rhodes Jackson. If anyone can provide knowledge of earliest publication source of this old story, or the author's next of kin, please send to Joe Wheeler (P.O. Box 1246, Conifer, CO 80433).

"Christmas in a Pickle Jar," by Emily Buck. Published in *The Christian Home*, December 1957 (The Graded Press, Nashville, Tennessee). Reprinted by permission of Abingdon Press, Nashville, Tennessee. If anyone knows the whereabouts of the author, or the author's next of kin, please contact Joe Wheeler (P.O. Box 1246, Conifer, CO 80433).

"The Bus Token," by Leland Mayberry. Published in *Sunshine Magazine*, December 1977. Reprinted by permission of Garth Henrichs of Sunshine Press.

"The Layaway Doll," by Marlene Chase. Published in *The War Cry*, Christmas 2005. Reprinted by permission of the author.

"Petronella," by Temple Bailey. If anyone can provide knowledge of the earliest publication source of this old story, or the whereabouts of the author's next of kin, please send to Joe Wheeler (P.O. Box 1246, Conifer, CO 80433).

"A Song for Elizabeth," by Robin Cole. Reprinted with permission from *Guideposts Magazine*. Copyright © 1979 by Guideposts, Carmel, New York 10512. All rights reserved.

"Flocks By Night," by Bruce Douglas. Published in *Country Gentleman*, December, 1938. Reprinted by permission of Farm Journal Media.

"A Cake of Pink Soap," author unknown. If anyone can provide knowledge of the author of this old story, or the author's next of kin, please contact Joe Wheeler (P. O. Box 1246, Conifer, CO 80433).

"A Very Special Present," by Ingrid Tomey. Published in *Woman's Day*, December 22, 1981. Reprinted by permission of the author.

"Bless the Child," by Isobel Stewart. Published in *Good Housekeeping*, December 1987. Reprinted by permission of the author.

"Star-spangled Christmas," by Kathleen Norris. Published in *Star-spangled Christmas*, Doubleday, 1940. If anyone knows the whereabouts of the author's next of kin, please send to Joe Wheeler (P.O. Box 1246, Conifer, CO 80433).

"Christmas Carol," by Margaret E. Sangster, Jr. Published in *The Girl's Companion*, December 13, 1946. Text printed by permission of Joe Wheeler (P.O. Box 1246, Conifer, CO 80433), and Cook Communications Ministries, Colorado Springs, CO.

"On Christmas Eve," by Helen Stökl. If anyone can provide knowledge of the author's next of kin or the earliest publication source of this old story, please send to Joe Wheeler (P.O. Box 1246, Conifer, CO 80433).

"The Mansion," by Henry Van Dyke. Published in *Harper's Monthly Magazine*, December 1910.

"Full Circle," by Lloyd Decker. If anyone can provide knowledge of the earliest publication source of this old story, or the whereabouts of the author's next of kin, please send to Joe Wheeler (P.O. Bos 1246, Conifer, CO 80433).

"Even When Nobody's Home," by Joseph Leininger Wheeler. Copyright © 2006. Reprinted by permission of the author. All rights reserved.

* * *

Contents

The Holy Night

We sate among the stalls at Bethlehem;
The dumb kine from their fodder turning them,
Softened their horned faces
To almost human gazes
Toward the newly Born:
The simple shepherds from the star-lit brooks
Brought their visionary looks,
As yet in their astonied hearing rung
The strange sweet angel-tonge:
The magi of the East, in sandals worn,
Knelt reverent, sweeping round,
With long pale beards, their gifts upon the ground,
The incense, myrrh, and gold
These baby hands were impotent to hold:
So let all earthlies and celestials wait
Upon thy royal state.
Sleep, sleep, my kingly One!

—Elizabeth Barrett Browning

Voices From the Past

Joseph Leininger Wheeler

I never cease to be amazed by God's incredible choreography, His perfect timing, in bringing mentors into our lives—just when we need them most. Many are living persons, and many lived long ago, but all of them still speak to us in the pages of books.

Epiphanies come to all of us, but sometimes we don't even recognize them while they're happening. Only in retrospect do we realize what their seismic impact has been on our lives know that if that particular day had never been, how different our lives would be today! This Christmas I'd like to share with you four mentors who dramatically changed my life—yet I never knew any of them outside the pages of books.

One day in particular stands out in memory.

A Spring Day on the Feather River

That Sabbath morning when I was 17, I was visiting my Aunt Jeanne and Uncle Warren Wheeler in Vina, California. The day was so heart-stoppingly beautiful that we decided to spend it along the Feather River—no particular agenda, other than finding the perfect picnic spot, strolling down to the river, talking, thinking, dreaming—and reading.

Earlier that week my aunt had taken me to the Tehama County Library and showed me the works of some of her favorite authors. Not for a second do I think it was coincidence that I chose Harold Bell Wright's *The Calling of Dan Matthews*. I had never heard of this author, but the title intrigued me.

And there, on a wild-flower-strewn knoll overlooking the swollen Feather River, I opened a book that would change the rest of my life. As a home-schooled child of missionary parents, I had been encouraged to read widely—and I had; often as many as 10 or 20 books a week. But never a book such as this!

God knew that glorious spring morning that I needed—almost desperately needed—a mentor who could provide me with new insights, new directions, and a purpose for the rest of my life. Let me tell you a little about the mentor who walked into my life that day.

* * *

Harold Bell Wright (1872-1944), born in Rome, New York, grew up poor and with few opportunities for schooling. The disease we today call tuberculosis attacked him early and plagued him for the rest of his life. He moved west to the Ozarks as a young man, searching for a drier climate and for answers to life's toughest questions. Though he had little education and no seminary training at all, he found himself pressed into service as an itinerant preacher with the Church of the Disciples. In the 12 years he would spend preaching in those hills, he was confronted with self-righteousness, narrow-thinking, doctrinaire controversies, feuds, ruthless ambition, intolerance, and letter-of-the-law rather than the spirit-of-the-law advocates, all common to denominations and churches everywhere in all times.

But it was Wright's good fortune to have been born into the seething cauldron of the Social Gospel Movement, evidenced in books such as Mary Augusta Ward's *Robert Elsmere* (1888) in England; and, eight years later, in America, Charles Sheldon's *In His Steps*. It was the perception that Christianity had become too rigid and legalistic, almost completely forgetting that the earthly ministry of Christ was virtually devoid of doctrine or legalism. Instead, He went about serving others, teaching, encouraging, and healing. And He never spoke without stories. The movement was especially strong in Congregational, Presbyterian, and Methodist churches.

Untrained though he was in theology, literature, or writing, Wright was nevertheless a born storyteller, able to create characters readers would strongly identify with. He would pick up where *In His Steps* left off with the three books we know today as The Social Gospel Trilogy: *That Printer of Udel's* (1903), *The Calling of Dan Matthews* (1909), and *God and the Groceryman* (1927). Thanks to Wright's relationship with The Book Supply Company of Chicago, his books sold by the millions, and he became one of the three most widely-read novelists in America.

For the very first time I perceived religion not as do's and don'ts but rather as an opportunity to part-ner with God in service for others. It was a dramatic shift for me, as I thereby gained a vision of an all-inclusive Lord who considered *all* of humankind—no matter where they lived, what faith they professed, or even if they professed none at all—as sheep He longed to bring into the fold. Furthermore, Wright wised me up to the insidious "throw-the-baby-out-with-the-bathwater" syndrome: "If Mr. Jones is a Christian, count me out, for he's a liar and a cheat." Wright introduced me to churches full of works in progress, such as myself, and revealed to me the fallacy of attempting to reform a church by throwing rocks through its windows from outside. *And that the devil is a master of the divide-and-conquer strategy.* He also pointed out that personal walks with God are possible, even for those who do not worship God in buildings.

I would go on to revel in *all* of Wright's books. In Texas, I shared the Wright "virus" with a neighbor. Much later she told me, "I cried last night because I read my last Wright book. Never again in life can I drink at the fountain of another of his books!"

* * *

As a 17-year-old, I had already read Charles Sheldon's *In His Steps* and been moved by it. Unlike Wright, **Charles Sheldon** (1857-1946), born in Wellsville, New York, was well educated. He was strongly impacted by Ward's *Robert Elsmere*, even before taking up Congregational pastorates in Waterbury, Vermont and Topeka, Kansas. Indeed, it was in Topeka that Sheldon wandered its streets disguised as a destitute man seeking work. It became quickly apparent to him that the churches in Topeka were the places least likely to extend a helping hand to those in need. But sermons about the problem fell on deaf ears.

Since so many pews were consistently empty during his Sunday evening services, he decided to write a book, having as its protagonist an out-of-work man seeking help. And following his Lord's example, he concluded that story would hold his audience's attention. It worked: no one wanted to miss even one chapter of the riveting story! A weekly newspaper picked it up, then hordes of book publishers both in America and around the world. Ironically, given that the message of the book could be reduced to four words, *What would Jesus do?* [were He in my shoes, faced with my decisions each day], most of those publishers pirated the book and paid its author nothing! However, thanks to those unscrupulous publishers, *In His Steps* became one of the age's most widely-read books. And Sheldon would go on to become editor of one of our greatest magazines, *Christian Herald*.

* * *

I was still an adolescent when I first read *The Story of the Other Wise Man*, by **Henry Van Dyke**. I have carried it in my heart ever since. Since my introduction to that story in *Christmas in My Heart 3* is so apropos to *The Mansion* in this collection, I am reaching back to draw from it . . .

For the 40-year-old scholar-cleric, Henry Van Dyke, 1892 had been a dark and tragic year during which his beloved father had died. The world saw merely the façade: Van Dyke at his peak—a graduate of Princeton, Princeton Theological School, and the University of Berlin; pastor of New York's prestigious Brick Presbyterian Church; author of such scholarly works as *The Poetry of Tennyson*. Yet inside he was anything but confident:

"*The year had been full of sickness and sorrow. Every day brought trouble. Every night was tormented with pain. They are very long—those nights when one lies awake, and hears the laboring heart pumping wearily at its task, and watches for the morning, not knowing whether it will ever dawn . . .*

"*And the heaviest burden?*

"*You must face the thought that your work in the world may be almost ended, but you know that it is not nearly finished. You have not solved the problems that perplexed you. You have not reached the goal that you aimed at. You have not accomplished the great task that you set for yourself. You are still on the way; and perhaps your journey must end now—nowhere—in the dark.*

"*Well, it was in one of these long, lonely nights that this story came to me. I have studied and loved the curious tales of the Three Wise Men of the East as they are told in the GOLDEN LEGEND of Jacobus de Voragine, and other medieval books. But of the Fourth Wise Man I had never heard until that night. Then I saw him distinctly, moving through the shadows in a little circle of light. His countenance was clear as the memory of my father's face as I saw it for the last time a few months before. The narrative of his journeyings and trials and disappointments ran without a break. Even certain sentences came to me complete and un-*

forgettable, clear-cut like a cameo. All that I had to do was to follow Artaban, step-by-step, as the tale went on, from the beginning to the end of his pilgrimage."

It is probable that more research went into this than any other Christmas story ever written. All his previous research, it appears in retrospect, had been setting the stage for this work. And now, it was not enough merely to tell the story he felt a Higher Power wished him to chronicle: it must have historical authenticity as well. So he scoured the great libraries of the world seeking information about every aspect of ancient life and travel. Not until he was satisfied that he knew his ground as well as an attorney presenting his first case before the Supreme Court did he finally begin writing.

What Van Dyke created was a story so simply and beautifully told that the reader is unaware that this recreation of the world our Lord knew is undergirded by prodigious research. It is an awesome tour de force.

On Christmas Day 1892, he spread out his manuscript on his pulpit, looked out at the vast hushed and expectant audience, and wondered how the Fourth Wise Man's story would be received. He needn't have worried: the little story spread like wildfire. Three years later, Harpers, the most prestigious publishing house in the world, launched it out across all the seas of the world, both in English and in many translations. I submit that as far as Christmas stories go, outside of Holy Writ, only Dickens' *Christmas Carol* is comparable in terms of power. The princely Artaban is proud and wants to impress God Himself by his munificence. Instead, he finds himself confronted with a series of great temptations, each packaged the same: *Shall I stay on schedule and join the Magi, or shall I stop and help this desperately needy person and risk the success of my life's greatest quest?* In each case, unwittingly, he mirrors the life of our Lord by choosing selfless service for others over self-gratification.

With *The Other Wise Man* already in the pantheon of "The Ten Greatest Christmas Stories Ever Written," Van Dyke followed it up 18 years later with a second, *The Mansion* (also published as a novelette-length book by Harpers). Sadly, though most well-read people are today knowledgeable about the first book, very few have ever heard of this one. A tragedy, for *The Mansion* is that rarity: a true life-changer. I know, for every time I read it I cringe, realizing once again how incredibly difficult it is to ever obliterate self-pride in oneself.

I must also admit that even though I am still a work-in-progress, *The Mansion* has made serious inroads into my self-pride, forcing me to qualify my answers to interviewers as I ascribe the credit to God rather than self. Revealing that the thoughts and insights they praise are not mine at all but God's, I pray The Prayer of Solomon every day I write, entreating God to grant me His divine wisdom, for my own is so shallow.

The Mansion is anything but a quick read! It must be read once then re-read periodically as long as we live, because it addresses the most insidious temptation the devil unleashes on us, one that comes at us so continually and in so many forms that we *never* gain the victory. All we can do is continue, humbly, to recognize that only with God's help do we even stand a chance at withstanding it.

* * *

I must not close this discussion without bringing in another of my mentors, **Lloyd C. Douglas** (1877-1951), born in Columbia City, Indiana. Although he was ordained as a minister in the Lutheran church, a number of his pastorates were in Congregational churches. A spiritual heir of Sheldon, Van Dyke, and Harold Bell Wright, Douglas's entire ministry had to do with showing how modern men and women may reflect the life and ministry of Christ in their every-day walk.

As was true with Wright, Sheldon, and Van Dyke, Douglas found that only a story was powerful enough to break through to the hearts of his parishioners. Over time he came to the conclusion that most people are "spiritually wistful," seeking ways in which they can grow, can become.

Douglas was 52 before he completed the book that is an extension of *The Mansion*. He titled it *Magnificent Obsession*. Published in 1929, it charts the story of Dr. Bobby Merrick, a brain specialist, who secretly practiced what he called "personality investments." In essence, the book depicts the life of a doctor who refuses to accept public credit for acts done in secret, his reason being that he'd already been recompensed inwardly by God. To belatedly be given credit in public would be tantamount to canceling out the spiritual blessing.

In Conclusion

So we do indeed learn much from mentors we never knew in person. Their voices continue to speak to us long after they are gone, a form of immortality, if you will. Had I the biographical data to draw from, I could discuss in like manner each of the several hundred authors who have already graced the pages of the *Christmas in My Heart* series.

Is not this special type of mentorship magical? How very much our lives are enriched by the likes of Harold Bell Wright, Charles Sheldon, Henry Van Dyke, and Lloyd C. Douglas!

The Sixteenth Collection

CODA

I look forward to hearing from you! Please do keep the stories, responses, and suggestions coming—and not just for Christmas stories. I am putting together collections centered on other genres as well. You may reach me by writing to:

Joe L. Wheeler, Ph.D.
P.O. Box 1246
Conifer, CO 80433

May the Lord bless and guide the ministry of these stories in your home.

When the Wise Man Appeared

William Ashley Anderson

He was cynical about God and religion, thus he laughed when his son Bruce came into the room carrying an ornate censor and wearing a long white nightgown, a purple cloak, and a crown made of yellow pasteboard and tinsel. Grudgingly, the father had agreed to take Bruce to the schoolhouse for the Christmas pageant.

The story takes place at the beginning of the twentieth century, when cars had to be cranked before they'd start. Part way to the school, the engine stopped. The rest of the story now begins.

For 15 years this story has haunted me. I now believe its time has come.

It was a bitterly cold night, vast and empty, a ringing void doomed with icy stars. Over Hallett's Hill the evening star danced like tinsel on the tip of a Christmas tree. The still air was resonant as the inside of an iron bell; but within our snug farmhouse it was mellow with the warmth of three cherry-red stoves. The dinner things had been pushed back, and I was feeling relaxed and content—when Bruce entered the room.

He was dressed in a long white nightgown with a purple cloak of Tintexed cotton over his shoulders. In one hand he held a tall crown of yellow pasteboard and tinsel. From the other swung an ornate censer. On his feet were thin, flapping sandals.

"What in the world are you supposed to be?" I laughed.

My wife looked at Bruce critically yet with concern and tenderness in her eyes. "He's one of the Wise Men of the East," she replied indignantly.

Her remark was an urgent reminder that I had promised to get Bruce to the schoolhouse in town in good time for the Christmas pageant. I shuddered and groaned at the thought of the cold and went out into the night pulling on a heavy coat, Bruce trailing after me.

The battery in the old car had gone dead, but by one of those freaks of mechanical whimsy that baffle man, its maker, the engine caught at the first turn of the crank, and off we went with a bang, bouncing and roaring across the rough frozen field. That was a trick of the devil, for at the turn by the barn the engine suddenly died. My heart sank. I looked out the side of my eyes at Bruce, sitting there, saying nothing, the crown and censer clasped in his arms, staring down that long endless lane that disappeared into the lonely hills.

It was a moment of deep breathless silence. The hills walled us in from all hope of neighborly assistance. Hallett's place was more than a mile and a half away, and the nearest turn of Route 90, even with the thin chance of a lift, was more than two miles away.

Well, I thought, *it's not tragically important.* Bruce

said nothing, but his eyes were wide, staring now at the big star twinkling just over the ragged edge of the mountain. Then a strange and uneasy feeling stirred in me, because I knew the boy was praying. He had made his promises, too, and he was praying that we would get to the schoolhouse in time for him to be one of the Three Wise Men.

I got out and strained and heaved at the crank, but it was useless. The still air cut like a knife. The cold metal clung to my hand. Every deep breath rasped my lungs until I sputtered. I rummaged through my pockets for my cigarettes. When I struck a light with fumbling hands and looked up through the smoke, Bruce was scuttling down the lane, one hand holding his skirts, one hand swinging the censer, the high golden crown perched cockeyed on his head. I hesitated between laughing at him and yelling for him to stop. I began once more to crank. Finally the engine began to cough throatily, and I scrambled frenziedly into the car.

Just about where Fifth Street enters Stroudsburg, I overtook Bruce. My heart went out to that small figure, trudging along with the cockeyed crown on his head and the censer hugged to his stomach. He turned his face into the lights with a white-lipped grin. His gown was torn, and he shivered violently.

"You shouldn't have gone off that way," I growled. "It's terribly cold!"

"I put twigs in the censer," he said, "and made a fire. I kept warm enough. I took a bearing on the star and made a short cut across Lasoine's farm. I came out right back there by the new cottage."

"But look at your feet! You might have frozen them!"

We arrived at the school on time. I stood in the back and watched.

A good many years had passed since I last saw the story of Bethlehem and the homage of the Three Wise Men presented by children at Christmastime. It had become so old a story to me that it seemed strange to realize that to them it was new.

When I saw Bruce, walking stiff-legged on cut and chilblained feet, with his two companions on the stage, kneeling by the crèche, declaiming his studied lines, I regretted my laughter at the dinner table, then an uneasy awe rose up within me I couldn't mull it out.

Going home, Bruce showed me where the short-cut came out.

"That's where the Thompsons lived," I said, "before the place burned down."

"I know," said Bruce. "Where the boy was burned to death."

As we passed the Lasoine farm there were lights burning. I thought this was strange, because since George Lasoine had gone off to war the old grandmother, who had lost her youngest son in the First World War, had sort of shriveled up, and a gloom lay over the house. But as I slowed down I could see Lou Lasoine through the kitchen window, smoking his pipe and talking with his mother and wife, and so I sensed everything was all right.

So far as I knew that was about all there was to the evening. But on Christmas Day, a farmer's wife, a neighbor of ours, came by with gifts of mincemeat made from venison, and a jug of sassafras cider. She had shaken off her customary pessimism and was full of bounce and high-pitched talk. She went into the kitchen where my wife was supervising the Christmas feast. Since I have a weakness for the racy gossip of the countryside, I drifted toward the kitchen too.

"You must hear this!" said my wife, drawing me in.

The farmer's wife looked at me with a glittering but wary eye. "You hain't a-goin' to believe it either," she said. "Just the same, I'm tellin' you, folks up here in the hills see things, and they do believe."

"What have you been seeing?"

"It was old Mrs. Lasoine. Last night when she was a-feelin' awful low she thought she heard something back of the barn and looked out. Now I'll say this for the old lady—she's got good vision. That she has! Plenty good! There warn't no moonlight, but if you recollect, it was a bright starry night. And there she saw, plain as her own husband, one of the Wise Men of the Bible come a-walkin' along the hill with a gold crown on his head, a-swingin' one of them pots with smoke in them—"

My mouth opened and I looked at Rosamunde, and Rosamunde looked at me, but before I could say anything, the woman hurried on:

"Now don't you start a-laughin'—not yet—'cause that hain't the long and the short of it! There's other testimony! Them Thompsons—you know the ones whose oldest boy was burned in a fire? Well, the children heard him first. They heard him a-singin' 'Come All Ye Faithful,' plain as day. They went runnin' to the window, and they seen the Wise Man a-walkin' in the starlight across the lane, gold crown and robes and fire-pot and all! Well, my goodness, they put up such a shoutin' and a yellin' that their parents come a-runnin'. But by then it was too late. He was gone. Just disappeared. Afterward they went out and looked, but they couldn't find hide nor hair—"

"Did they see any other signs?" I asked faintly.

The farmer's wife scoffed. "Old folks and children see things which maybe we can't. All I can say is this: Lasoines and Thompsons don't even know each other. But old lady Lasoine was heartsick and lonely and a-prayin' about her lost boy, and the Thompsons was heartsick and lonely because this was the first Christmas in the new house without Harry, and you dasn't say they wasn't a-prayin' too! Maybe you don't believe that amounts to anythin'—but I'm tellin' you it was a comfort to them to see and believe!"

I swallowed hard, recalling the look on Bruce's face as he stared at the star, when I knew he was praying that he might not fail his friends. Well, not daring to look at my wife, I said with all the sincerity I can feel: "Yes, I believe God was close last night."

The farmer's wife looked at me in disbelief, for she knew I was not a very religious person. She stared as if an even greater miracle had been performed before her very eyes.

Christmas in the Street of Memories

Elizabeth Rhodes Jackson

The children were curious. It was getting colder and colder yet the supposedly rich Mrs. Lavendar was shivering in her almost empty house. They decided to find out why.

Children everywhere have so taken this story to heart that they consider it unthinkable not to listen to it every Christmas of their lives.

The Prince and Princess live with Mr. Lifsky on the street floor, we live on the next floor, and old Mrs. Lavendar lives on the top floor.

We first got acquainted with Mrs. Lavendar by accident. The accident happened to Beany.

There are three of us. Jack is my older brother, and Beany is my younger brother. I am Dee, and I am just 11.

We live on one of the oldest streets in Boston, at the foot of Beacon Hill. The houses have alleys at the back or through their cellars, and we play tag in them. The al-leys all run into each other and make a sort of maze. You run up an alley and climb over a couple of fences and down another alley and through a gate, and there you are in another street. We were all playing one day after school, and Beany went to climb a fence and fell, right on his face. Beany would, you know. He's always the one of us that has the falls. He bruised his forehead and skinned his nose. He was very brave about it and didn't cry, although the tears were in his eyes.

We took him home, Jack and I, but when we took Beany upstairs to our landing, the door was locked and Mother was out. Beany had been brave so long that he couldn't wait any longer, and while I was fumbling in the regular place for the key, he burst out into a long, sad wail. Then a lady on the floor above, who was a stranger to us, leaned over the banister and said, "Bring him up to me."

Her apartment was very lovely with beautiful, old furniture; and soft, thick rugs on the floor; and huge silver candlesticks on the mantel. But there was no fire in the fireplace, though the day was cold, and she had on a beautiful white silk shawl with an embroidered border. She took Beany on her lap and washed the dirt off his face very gently. Then she held him in her arms, and we sat on the rug and she told us about her son when he was a little boy.

That was how we got acquainted with Mrs. Lavendar. And that was the way we came to find the Prince and the Princess.

Mother calls the street we live on the Street of Memories, for two reasons. One is that memories of the past are still living there. Two blocks from our house, at the corner of Boston Common, is the spot where the British soldiers embarked the night that Paul Revere got ahead of them on his famous ride. Two blocks the other way, Oliver Wendell Holmes used to live. And Miss Alcott walked on our street many and many a time. I love to walk up the hill to see the little brick house where she and her sister kept house—Jo and Amy—in their struggling days, and on the way home I pass the stately mansion (Dr. Holmes said that in "The Chambered Nautilus"), where she lived when she was successful and famous.

The other reason Mother calls it the Street of Memories is because of the antique shops all up and down the street. Some of them are very artistic, with nothing but two colonial chairs and a table in the window. But we like best the ones that have the windows crowded full of new and interesting things. Mr. Lifsky's is like that, on the street floor of our house. His show window is just jammed with three ship models and some colored bottles, a battered old lantern, and andirons and silhouettes in tiny frames, and an inlaid snuff box, and a pair of china dogs, and a luster tea set; and hanging up are old engravings and faded samplers.

We were all three looking into Mr. Lifsky's window one day when Mrs. Lavendar came out and saw us there. We knew her very well by that time.

"Mrs. Lavendar, do see this ship's model," said Jack.

"It looks like all sorts of adventures," she said, and then she caught her breath a little.

"How long have those been here?" she said. "I haven't seen them before."

She was pointing to a pair of china figures, a lady and gentleman in elaborate old-fashioned dress. The lady had wide skirts and high powdered hair and flowers on her breast, and the gentleman had a ruffled shirt and knee breeches and buckled shoes. They were tiny but very perfect and delicate, and the faces were exquisitely beautiful.

"I'm sure those are mine," said Mrs. Lavendar, very low. Then she walked into Mr. Lifsky's shop.

"She's going in to buy them," we said, but presently she came out without them.

We told Mother about it. "Why do you think she didn't buy them?" asked Jack.

"Probably Mr. Lifsky's price was too high," said Mother.

"Oh, but Mrs. Lavendar is rich," said Beany. "You ought to see her beautiful apartment."

"I'm afraid she's not," said Mother. "She used to have a great deal of money, but now she is old and poor and alone. Her son lost his life in the war, you know."

"I wonder if that's why she doesn't have a fire in the fireplace," I said, for we often went up to see her now, and her apartment was usually cold. Of course, the house is supposed to be heated from the cellar, but we always have two log fires going in winter to help out. Our house is a beautiful old residence that has been made over into apartments, so the plumbing and heating are old-fashioned and often cause us trouble.

A week later we had cold weather. Cold weather in Boston is *very* cold. I don't believe even the North Pole is any colder than the Street of Memories in winter!

"I was going to suggest you going up to see Mrs. Lavendar," said Mother, when we came home from school, "but it is so cold, perhaps you'd better take a fire with you."

I followed her up the stairs and heard her saying, "Mrs. Lavendar, would it bother you if the children made a little call?"

"I'd love to have them," said Mrs. Lavendar, "only I'm afraid the room is rather cold. I can't seem to get enough heat."

"It's a frightful heating system, isn't it?" said Mother. "We've had to have a hearth fire today. Jack will bring up some wood, if you don't mind the litter."

So soon we were on the way up, Jack with a basket of logs, Beany carrying the paper bag of kindling, and I with the hearth brush. Beany, poor child, tripped over the rug and dropped the bag, which split open, but Mrs. Lavendar was very nice about it, and I swept up the debris and it was all right. Jack made a glorious fire, and we were very cozy. Knowing Mother, I suspect she planned the whole thing just to get Mrs. Lavendar warm.

While we were all sitting there, as happy as could be, Beany suddenly spoke up. Beany too frequently says things he shouldn't, and what he said this time was "Mrs. Lavendar, how did your china figures come to be in Mr. Lifsky's antique shop?"

We tried to hush him, but Mrs. Lavendar said, "I sold all the furnishings of my house some years ago, except what I have here, and the little Prince and Princess went with the rest."

"Are they a Prince and Princess?" I asked.

"That was the name my boy had for them when he was little." And somehow, from the way she said it, I knew that she missed the little china figures.

Then Beany piped up again. "Why did you have to sell your furniture, Mrs. Lavendar, when you have so much money?"

We couldn't hush him at all, but Mrs. Lavendar understood, and she only smiled and said, "I haven't much money, dear. I had some, but it was taken from me. So I had to sell the furniture to get money to live on."

"How was it taken?" said Beany, all interest.

"It isn't a very pleasant story," said Mrs. Lavendar. "My investments were in a business that could not go on until the war was over."

Beany nodded, though he didn't understand. We did, partly.

"My son's salary was enough for us till he went to war. Then we planned to sell our house and invest the money to take care of me till he came back."

"I see," said Beany.

"My son came in with the money from the sale one afternoon. He wouldn't take a check because sometimes checks can't be collected. He went to the bank with the man who bought the house, and the man drew out the money in bills and gave it to him—$40,000. It was too late to take the money to my bank for deposit that day, so he brought it home to me, and it was taken that same day."

"Who took it?" we asked together.

"I never knew," said Mrs. Lavendar. "Not the servants. They had been with me for years. Someone must have come in—but I don't know how. It has always been a mystery."

"Where was it?" we asked.

"In the Governor Winthrop desk," said old Mrs.

Lavendar, "that very desk there against the wall. My son said, 'I'll put it in here, Mother.' I saw him with his hand on the open leaf of the desk. I said, 'Yes, that's a perfectly safe place.' I went out to see my son off then, and I was so confused and troubled over parting with him that I forgot to lock it. And when I went to get the money next day to take it to the bank, it was not there."

"This very desk!" said Jack. We were all very much excited, for we knew that some of those old desks have secret drawers and false backs to the pigeonholes. It seemed perfectly clear to us that there were $40,000 somewhere inside that solid square old piece of mahogany, and if we could find it, Mrs. Lavendar would be rich again. We told her so very excitedly, but she shook her head.

"I've known this desk all my life, my dears," she said. "It was my great-grandfather's. I know every nook and corner of it. It has no secrets."

"May we look through it?" we said. "We might be able to find *something*."

Of course, Mrs. Lavendar let us, and we took out all the papers and the drawers, and measured and tapped and pushed to find secret springs. But we had to give it up at last. If the money was still there, hidden in some secret place, it was too successfully hidden for us to find.

I noticed that the beautiful silver candlesticks were not on the mantel, and Mrs. Lavendar was wearing a little black sweater instead of the embroidered shawl. I was afraid Beany would notice and ask if she had to sell them, too, but he

was too interested in the desk to ask questions about anything else.

For several days we talked about the money, and then we forgot all about it for a while because of Christmas. We were busy as could be, writing our Christmas wants and making things and counting our savings and going shopping for presents after school. We all painted cards for Mrs. Lavendar, of course, and it was while we were doing this, one snowy day, that I said, "Oh, dear; I wish we could buy the Prince and Princess and give them to Mrs. Lavendar for Christmas!"

"That's just like you, Dee," said Jack. "One of those brilliant ideas that there's no way of carrying out!"

I knew he didn't mean that to sound unpleasant. It was just that he wanted so much to do it, and didn't see how we could.

"Let's ask Mr. Lifsky how much they are, anyway!" said Beany.

Beany is always so hopeful. Jack and I knew it was useless, because we had already spent all our money for Christmas. But Beany went down to ask Mr. Lifsky and came back soon to tell us.

"Seven dollars and fifty cents." He said it just as cheerfully as if we had $7.50 right there.

And then something very unexpected happened. We were playing tag in the back alley a few days later, and by mistake we tipped over an ash barrel. When we went to pick up the junk we had spilled, we found some old bundles of letters, tied with faded ribbon and photographs, and some good camera films. Someone had just moved out of the house, and there was no one there but a cleaning woman. We showed her the films and asked if we could have them, and she said we could have anything we found in the back yard, but we must clean up any rubbish we spilled. There were four or five barrels in the yard, and we dumped them all out, one after another, and found a number of very worthwhile articles. But the really important thing was two filled books of trading stamps, and when we saw those, we knew, after all, that there was hope of our buying the Prince and Princess.

We took the stamps home to Mother, and she said they were worth $2 for each book and that it would be all right for Jack to go and get the money for them, as otherwise they would be burned for rubbish. So while Jack hurried off across the Common to the department stores, Beany and I went back to dig again for buried treasure. We didn't find anything else in the barrels, but Beany spied a row of store milk bottles, and we gathered those up and took them back to the chain store. There were 21 of them, and that gave us $1.05, so when Jack came back with the trading stamp money, we had $5.05, altogether.

"Perhaps Mr. Lifsky would come down," said Jack. "People always do bargain for antiques, you know."

So we took the five $1 bills and the nickel and showed them to Mr. Lifsky. We told him that was all the money we had and asked if he would sell us the pair of china figures. We couldn't pay another cent for them.

"For fife tollars und fife cents you ask it!" said Mr. Lifsky indignantly. "Ten times ofer could I sell them little fickures for fife tollars und fife cents! Seven-fifty ist mine price, und not one cent less than fife-fifty."

"We haven't got five-fifty," said Jack.

"Fife-fifty!" Mr. Lifsky said again, so we went out to talk it over.

"We almost have it," said Jack. "Only 45 cents. Let's all think hard."

So we all thought hard. But it was Beany who thought of asking Mother to advance 45 cents of our pocket money. There was a great shout of joy from us all when he came back with it. We went right into Mr. Lifsky's and bought the Prince and Princess. They were a little bit dusty, and Jack thought we ought to put them into the bathtub and wash them. But Mother thought not, because we might chip them or wash off the color, and Mrs. Lavendar would know best how to clean them. Then we started to wrap them in Christmas paper, but we were afraid that Mrs. Lavendar might break them in opening them. Besides it would be more fun to have her see them right away, the minute she opened the door.

Jack wanted to be the one to carry the Prince, and I wanted to carry the Princess, and Beany felt very bad about it.

"It's just because I'm the youngest," he said. "I have to take turns with you filling the wood basket and going to the store, but no one ever takes turns with me being the youngest. I thought how to get the last 45 cents, anyway. And Mrs. Lavendar was my friend first."

So we told him he could be the one to say, "Merry Christmas, Mrs. Lavendar; we've brought you a present." So it was settled.

* * *

Christmas Eve is very beautiful on Beacon Hill. All the houses are lighted with candles in every window, and the curtains are drawn back so that everyone can see the inside. The houses are all very beautiful to see, too, because most of them were built in the early days and have winding staircases and paneled walls, and many of them have beautiful tapestries and paintings. A great crowd comes from all over Boston, so that you can hardly move through the streets, but everyone is quiet and reverent. It is almost like church outdoors, especially after the carols begin. Mother always takes us out for a little while, after we have lighted the candles in our own windows.

This Christmas Eve we asked Mrs. Lavendar to go out with us, but she thought she might get too tired. So when we came back, we three sang carols just for her, "Silent Night, Holy Night" and "The First Noel"— looking up at the candles in her windows.

It is such an exciting feeling to wake on Christmas morning and see the stockings all lumpy. But this Christmas I had a 'specially joyous feeling, and I remembered we were going to take the Prince and Princess to Mrs. Lavendar.

Right after breakfast we went upstairs, Jack carrying the Prince and I carrying the Princess, just as we had planned. But halfway upstairs I caught a glimpse of Beany's face. He had a scratch across his chin where the grocer's cat had scratched him when he tried to pet her, and he had such a sad look that I was sorry for him. It must be hard to be the youngest. So I said, "Here, Beany, you can carry her," and handed him the Princess.

We got to the top of the stairs, and Jack looked around and saw how it was, and he said, "Oh, well," and he put the Prince into my hands. So after all it was Jack who lifted the brass knocker and said, "Merry Christmas, Mrs. Lavendar; we've brought you a present."

But when she saw the Prince and Princess, she said, "Oh, you *dear* children!" very softly.

Then she said, "Their home is on the desk, dears, one on each side of my son's picture."

I walked across the room and put the Prince on the desk very carefully, and Beany came next. But then Beany slipped, and down he came, *crash!* on the floor. Beany *would!*

Mrs. Lavendar stooped over the pieces.

"I am sure we can mend the Princess," she was saying, and then she gasped and picked up something from under the pieces.

It was a roll of bills that had been inside the hollow Princess.

"The money was not taken," she said slowly. "It was there all the time!" She sat down, and her hands were trembling. "I begin to understand," she said. "My son was standing by the desk. I never thought of the Princess. But of course he would put it there. From the time he was a baby he used to stow all sorts of little treasures through that hole in the base. He thought of course that I saw him putting it there and that no one else would know."

* * *

We had a great rejoicing after that, and since then Mrs. Lavendar hasn't gone out to do sewing any more. The silver candlesticks are back on the mantel, and she wears the white silk shawl, and has a fire, too, on cold days. And she has mended the Princess with china cement so you can't see the cracks at all unless you get up very close.

Christmas in a Pickle Jar

Emily Buck

Mary was plumb discouraged. Everything that could go wrong in the Christmas program rehearsal had, from the narrator with the croupy cough to the condescending college girl director to the scratchy playing of the viola player to the aged soprano who could no longer hit the high notes. The program was a guaranteed disaster.

Or was it?

Corrugated cardboard and old pickle jars, thought Mary as she stared distastefully at the back of the crèche that had been set up on the edge of the low stage in the community center. *My view of Christmas!*

Arranging her music on the piano behind the crèche, she was vaguely aware of the uneven rows of folding chairs beginning to fill with townspeople, most of whose faces were quite familiar to Mary—many housewives like herself.

What have they come for? Mary wondered. Did they expect to find even a fragment of the Christmas spirit here, at a program of carols by the churches of the community, so inexpertly presented by an assortment of small-town talent—from a vocalizing grandmother with wandering capabilities to an unskilled brass choir of boys that included her own son, David?

This would be the first time David and she had ever been remotely connected to any public performance, and she was all too acutely aware of the shame that would be his if her part did not go well. All she could do now, however, was hope to play her best. As far as the Christmas spirit went, it must find its way to her some other night.

Her glance wandered to the jar nearest her. "Crisp Sweet Pickles," she read.

The pickle jars, weighted with sand, held small evergreens in a feeble decorative attempt. And on the audience side of the corrugated backing must be the shepherds and Wise Men, although she couldn't be sure, since the crèche had not been here for rehearsal yesterday.

Mary winced as she recalled that rehearsal.

The narrator, a sweet-voiced lady who suffered terribly from headaches, had been plagued in addition by a croupy cough. But she had started off bravely enough, reading the commentary that led up to the first number, an Indian pantomime to be put on by a group of little Girl Scouts.

At the proper moment, the self-assured young college girl who had been oh-so-gracefully instructing the Scouts for the past three Saturdays, stepped forward. "How's about doing our Indian number? OK?" She had smiled with false encouragement, and the little girls had attempted to line up on the floor in front of the stage.

"Remember, there's a short intro, and then you start. OK?" And she nodded brightly at Mary to begin.

Mary began her introduction (three rehearsals with the young college girl had not sufficed to make her feel at ease calling it an "intro"), hearing again in an odd flash of memory how the college girl had introduced her the previous Saturday to her boyfriend: "This is my piano player," she had said. And Mary had managed to smile politely as though a great honor had been conferred upon her.

The Scouts struggled valiantly. Mary could see them out of the corner of her eye, could hear and feel their heavy feet shaking the floor as she played through their number. But when she came to the end there was a strange silence. No one said anything, and with a sudden hot feeling Mary looked more carefully at the page she had been playing, then at the one opposite.

"I'm very sorry," she said, her face burning as she tried to avoid the eyes of her son and his friends. "I played the wrong carol."

The silence eased a trifle, and Mary proceeded to play successfully through the right one. *But why, Mary raged inwardly, why didn't anyone stop me before? Why let me go through the whole wrong piece without saying anything?*

At the conclusion of the Indian number there was a disturbance at the back of the hall, and the minister's wife, who was director and coordinator of the rather ambitious program, came forward. She commanded everyone's attention.

"No, no," she said, her brow puckered in a worried frown. "They should not finish facing the audience. At the performance tomorrow night we are going to have a crèche there on the front of the stage. And since this is supposed to be a pantomime of worship, they should end up just the other way, toward the crèche."

"OK."

Could nothing ruffle that young college girl?

"How's about doing your last bit going in a half circle like this, girls?" She bent her supple curves and gave a sketchy run-through while the little Girl Scouts watched uncomprehendingly.

"OK?" She smiled winningly. "I'm sure you'll do that just fine. Now you're excused."

You mean, Mary almost spoke aloud, *you're not going to have them go through that new part at all? You expect them to get it just from* that?

But the Scouts were done, and it was a relief to everyone to have their noise and bustle leave. Then, after a few brief sentences from the narrator, attention turned to the brass choir who was to play intermittently for the various carols the audience was supposed to sing. Mary knew from David that the boys had been able to work in only one skimpy rehearsal and were not really prepared at all. And the first hair-raising blasts provided plenty of proof.

The music director of one of the churches, a husky, intense young man, who might well have dedicated himself to football rather than music, looked pained and stopped them abruptly.

The minister's wife, taking advantage of the break, asked him, "Do you want the piano to play with you?"

"No," he said, shaking his head wearily, "she's not in the same key." He surveyed his group and added, with pale humor, "Of course *we're* not in the same key, either. Come on, fellows, you can do better than that!"

A soprano solo came next. The singer was a housewife-turned-working-mother, whose oldest daughter was away at an expensive college. She looked tired, and her voice broke on several of the higher notes. Mary felt sorry for her—she seemed so discouraged as she sat down.

Another explanatory interlude from the narrator, another attempt by the brasses, and so the rehearsal had gone on. When it came time for the contralto solo, there was none. The tall young mother had already had to leave.

"She's nursing her baby, you know," the soprano explained.

The narrator turned a page and went on, although her taut face and dull eyes indicated that her headache must be reaching a peak of pain.

When the time came for the viola selection, that lady had lost her place in following the program, so was quite unprepared. And the minutes had dragged while she took her viola out of its case, then repeatedly tuned and tested each string—a meticulous process quite uncalled for in the light of the scratchy and inaccurate performance that followed.

The final blow was delivered precisely as Mary had been dreading it. This was the soprano solo sung by the grandmother. In days gone by she had done much concert singing of the operatic variety, but in recent years had *talked* at length about practicing without doing any.

From their one prior rehearsal together, Mary was tensed ahead of time, awaiting the climax where the voice part took off to a high B-flat—which the good lady could not possibly reach.

Mary felt the others cringe with her as the hall echoed harshly to that wavering note, and she wished with all her heart that somehow she could find the courage to suggest that the poor lady take the lower B-flat so clearly marked in the music as a possible substitute. But how could she, tactfully?

After the rehearsal, Mary had walked home through the winter dark in a tired and depressed state that had not been helped by David's remarks as he stamped in the door some time later.

"It was *terrible!*" he announced flatly, slamming his trumpet case in its corner by the piano. "The whole thing! We played so hard we got all dry, and our lips are practically shot!"

So that was the program of Christmas carols all these people were coming to hear—and the hall really was filling up. Mary gazed in growing astonishment past the fence of corrugated cardboard in front of her.

Over in the corner David and the other boys had already settled their music stands, practically in the branches of a large Christmas tree that had been set up since yesterday's rehearsal. Lined up in the front row were all the little Scouts. On the stage beside her the soloists had taken their places, and in the opposite corner from the boys sat the narrator beside another tall tree.

All was ready, and as the minister's wife rose and began her introductory remarks, Mary knew that nothing could now stop the program. It was about to begin.

Afterward, Mary found she could recall the exact moment when the change took place. It was well past the beginning, for then she had been too keyed up remembering to play the right piece for the Scouts and their Indian number to think of anything else. But there had come a breather in the program, an interval when the narrator took over at some length.

Mary had felt her tenseness slip away, and she had looked out over the audience, her eyes coming finally to rest on the trombone player in the brass choir. A branch of the Christmas tree was almost touching his cheek, and a strand of shiny tinsel hung down over one broad shoulder. She saw him suddenly as he had looked years ago as a small Cub Scout, one of her den that had so faithfully come to her each week.

Untrained but willing, she had done her best, and they all had found it rewarding, Cubs and den mother alike. And as Mary's gaze went from the trombone player to her own son, David, to the other boys and the soloists, she knew instantly that they were doing their best too, right this very minute—and the audience was satisfied.

For the little Girl Scouts in the front row, looking so neat in their white blouses, the pantomiming had been fun; and who had minded their mistakes and confusions? The soprano who worked so hard, helping send a daughter to college, had sung a well-loved carol; and her friends and neighbors had enjoyed listening. After all, they had not come expecting to hear professional concert artists.

The narrator now paused. It was time for the contralto solo.

The tall young mother stood up, beautiful and serene—she had somehow worked out her baby's schedule so she could be there. "I wonder as I wander," she sang, her voice warm and sure as it flowed out over the audience. And Mary knew that the rest of the program would be as gratifying.

It was. The viola lady remembered just when her turn came. Her piece went smoothly; and indeed, Mary realized it was rightly a matter of pride in the community that so small a place could boast a viola player. The audience, under the stimulation of the brass choir's unexpectedly mellow accompaniment, sang with all their hearts. And for a fitting conclusion, the grandmother gently and gracefully ended her song on the lower B-flat.

With a grateful sigh, Mary collected her music and left the stage. Emerging from the side door by the Christmas tree and the brass choir, she found David and the other boys in a flurry of packing up instruments—refreshments had been announced to be served immediately.

He glanced up quickly. "It went OK," he said, his smile both pleased and surprised.

"You all did beautifully," Mary agreed.

"And you played swell, Mom!"

With a snap, he shut his trumpet case and was off to the ice cream and punch before Mary could collect herself enough to realize that her own son had just given her the nicest compliment that she could ever possibly receive from him.

She turned to watch him, but instead found herself in front of the crèche. There were the shepherds and Wise Men, as she had guessed, the animals, and the Holy Family so quietly radiant. No sign of the corrugated cardboard—and where had the pickle jars gone?

Only the little trees showed, tucked in by sprays of evergreen boughs.

Mary stood for a moment, wondering. How long ago had it been that she had sat, staring so irritably at Crisp Sweet Pickles?

It did not matter. The Christmas spirit was here; her view it was that had changed.

The Bus Token

Leland Mayberry

Jenny was angry with her mother for not buying her that watch she so longed for. After all, it only cost about $100.

Then, outside a store window, she heard a small boy's voice.

Jenny stared unseeingly at the bright Christmas display in the store window. Crowds of hurrying shoppers surged around her, but she didn't see or hear them. Her mind was awhirl with disturbing thoughts. Why couldn't her parents understand even her most simple wish? Why couldn't she have been an only child without the handicap of three younger brothers? Surely a teenage daughter should count for something. But no, the entire family picked on her.

I get good grades in school, she thought rebelliously. *Better than Jim and John and Jerry. And I keep my own room neat—well, almost. I help with the dishes and baby-sit sometimes. Why can't I have that watch?*

With tightened lips she remembered her mother's words.

"Jenny, you have a watch, and I see no reason to get you another. We have the boys to think of, too. We simply cannot manage to pay almost $100 for something you think you want."

"But Mom, I'm not asking for anything else for Christmas. Just this watch. It's beautiful, Mom. The bracelet is really neat. No one else at school has one, and I could be the first. Besides, it's practical. You can't tell it's a watch until you press a button and the time shows. It tells the month and the day, too."

"No, Jenny," her mother had said with unexpected firmness. "There will be no watch for Christmas."

Jenny turned from the bright lights of the store window and buttoned her coat. She wished the bus would come. She was wasting her time here, but a store window was better than listening to her mother's unreasonable scolding. But she ought to get home and start on her lessons.

A small boy with a gray stocking cap pushed by her. He exclaimed in a shrill voice, "Look, Ma! There's the car I want. Do you think I could have that car for Christmas?" He pointed a grubby finger at the toy in the window.

Jenny looked down at the child then at the toy which had prompted his excitement. She saw a tiny, inexpensive red automobile with rubber wheels and shining fenders.

The mother's voice was soft and tired. "But son, it costs 59 cents!" She spoke as if the amount were an absolute impossibility.

I wish I could get him the car, Jenny thought. *Poor little kid! He looks as if he has no toys.*

The boy continued staring at the bright red car, nose pressed against the window. He stood close to Jenny, and she resisted an impulse to smooth his jacket collar. Her fingers tightened around her small purse.

Why can't I give him the car? she asked herself. *I've probably got the money with me now.*

Almost reluctantly, she counted her coins—four dimes, three pennies, and a bus token. Forty-three cents was not enough. She was surprised at her disappointment. *Let's see . . . The streetcar costs 59 cents, and the tax would make it sixty-two. I need 19 more cents,* she calculated quickly.

The bus token! But she would have to walk home in the cold and wind. It would be a long walk. Her hesitation was brief. She separated the token from the dimes and pennies. Holding it between two fingers as if it were treasure, she walked into the store.

"Hello, Jenny," the man behind the counter hailed her. "Something I can do for you today?"

"Mr. Grimes, how much will you give me for this bus token?" She held it out.

"A bus token, huh? Well, I'll tell you, Jenny. I need to get home tonight, and I go by bus." He laughed at his own little joke.

"I'll sell it to you, Mr. Grimes."

"The regular fare is 25 cents. I'll give you 20 cents for the token."

"I'll take it," she said, and he handed her two dimes. She turned to see if the little boy and his mother were still there, his button nose pressed against the window, his eyes caressing the toy which could never be his.

"Mr. Grimes," she said hurriedly, "I want to buy a car like the one in the window for 59 cents. I'm in a hurry."

"OK, Jenny." He brought out a little box which he opened. "Is this the one?"

She nodded.

"You don't usually do your Christmas shopping here, do you? That will be 62 cents, counting the tax."

She handed him the two dimes he had exchanged for the bus token. Added to them were her own four dimes and two pennies.

"Thank you, Mr. Grimes. 'Bye." Clutching the packaged toy, she almost ran from the store.

The woman and the boy were turning slowly to leave. He cast a last longing look at the toy in the window.

"Wait, wait!" called Jenny.

They stopped uncertainly as she approached them.

"Here," Jenny said breathlessly as she thrust her purchase into the boy's chilled hands. "A Christmas present, for you." She turned and hurried around the corner.

The walk home seemed but a short distance to Jenny. She breathed the cold crisp air in hungry lungfuls. She carefully read the faces of passersby, something she had never done before. She found herself wondering about their homes and family circumstances, their joys and sorrows. She thought about the child with the new toy. *First time I've ever done anything for anyone outside my family*, she told herself. She wondered at the strange exhilaration she felt. It was as if she were newborn.

When she reached home, she found herself running up the front steps with unaccustomed gladness. Her mother, dusting furniture in the hall, turned at her entrance.

"Hi, Mom," said Jenny. "I walked home. Had some thinking to do."

She noted her mother's pleased surprise when she took the dust cloth from her hands and began polishing an invisible spot on a small table. "Mom, I've decided something," she said. "I don't want that watch after all. I don't need it."

Smiling at her mother's obvious relief, she added thoughtfully, "I've already had my Christmas."

The Layaway Doll

Marlene Chase

She was angry, bitter, and cold. Success itself was but ashes in her mouth. All her money could not buy her lost daughter or the love of her family, her family that was slipping away.

So she was rude to the young, green-eyed widow, unfeeling, abrupt.

But after the brokenhearted young woman fled . . .

A blast of wintry air and the tinkle of the old-fashioned bell alerted Sharon Conroy that someone had entered the store. Less than eager to face another last-minute Christmas shopper, she took her time arranging some boxes on the lower shelf.

That tinkling bell had heralded patrons for nearly 25 years, and the scent of bayberry from fancy candles interspersed among the trinkets and accessories of Conroy's Doll Company were tediously familiar. As she lingered beneath the counter, it was as if her whole life were suddenly freeze-framed in a dull brown malaise. Could feeling this way have something to do with her conversation that morning with her son? Children could be so selfish, so ungrateful at times.

"I'm sorry, Mom," he'd said, "but we just can't make it this year. Cindy's folks are expecting us early—and with the storm coming—" Sharon had swallowed the disappointment that left a bitter aftertaste. Why was it children had so little time for parents who had fed and clothed them, who had sacrificed to give them the best years of their lives? Sharon's granddaughter, Kelly, would have her pick of the doll collection, a gift worth hundreds. Most 8-year-olds could only dream of possessing such a collection, but then most children don't have one of the country's premier doll designers for a grandma. *You'd think they'd realize how expensive . . .*

The pain in her ankles brought her back to the moment, and she rose to find herself looking into the face of a young woman, a mere girl really, who'd become a familiar visitor every week.

"Oh, I'm so glad you didn't close early!" came the breathless greeting. "I want to pay the balance on my doll."

The girl's faded jacket and dirty tennis shoes, her mousey hair tugging out of its pony tail, set her apart from the successful women who frequented Conroy's. Sharon gripped the edge of the mahogany counter as the green eyes, which she had often reflected were notably the girl's best feature, danced like green bubble lights. The girl flung back the hood of a dilapidated jacket, releasing a fine wet spray. "I have it here . . ." She pulled the strap of her purse over her thin shoulder and began rifling through its contents.

"The doll . . . Yes."

"Isn't it exciting? Snow—and just in time for Christmas!" The compelling green eyes seemed to glow even brighter. Sharon grimaced at the white flurry against the glass. Traffic at the Corners would be murder. She took a deep breath as her young patron gushed on about Christmas, and snow, and how she couldn't wait to take the doll home. She had looked just the same the first time she'd come into the shop.

"The angel doll," she had said, her voice secretive, though she'd been alone, and no one else was near. "It's the one my little girl wants. She can't stop talking about it, and I really want to get it for her. I can pay, a little at a time, until Christmas."

Sharon had sized up the skinny twentysomething in the blue and white Hadley Inn uniform. That hotel hired mainly high school dropouts and foreigners, and from the look of this girl, they didn't pay very well. She'd raised her eyebrows when the girl asked about "Celeste," the only angel among Conroy's collectors' dolls.

"We were passing, Emma and me," the young woman had said, "and we saw the doll, and from that very minute my Emma just had to have it."

People today, Sharon had thought bitterly. *They had to have everything their eyes lit on, regardless what it cost.* When she'd told the girl that the Celeste angel doll cost $250, she had blinked twice rapidly but said softly, "Can you put it on layaway, and I'll pay a little every week?"

Layaway indeed! What did she think this was, Wal-Mart? Would a child even know the difference between a handcrafted doll and the mass-produced model at a fraction of the cost? But the girl had only smiled and come faithfully every Friday since the first of November, with $28, one of eight weekly installments, clutched in her cheap plastic purse.

Sharon sighed and went to retrieve the doll, the "Celeste." It was her least favorite. She was glad it was the only one left. *Silly to let children think there were such things as angels. All that nonsense about a God in heaven and angels that watched over them. The angels had been pretty scarce when Karin had*—Sharon stopped herself. She had determined long ago not to go down that self-pity road. But Christmas seemed to bring it all back. Well, she'd picked up the pieces and done the best she could for Kevin. She'd worked hard to give him the best of everything. Weekends, evenings, whatever it took. She'd been certain he had it all. But somehow it hadn't been enough. Kevin barely visited anymore, and he was a scant 75 miles away. He wasn't even going to make it for Christmas Eve.

Sharon set the box down in front of the girl. The dull thump it made echoed the little angry nerve in the back of her mind. She grabbed a pen and the invoice pad as the girl lifted the lid of the box and gently pulled back the tissue.

"Oh," she whispered reverently. "She is so beautiful—as beautiful as the angel over Bethlehem when Jesus was born, Emma says."

Sharon looked away, embarrassed. The child had never come in with her mother. What had she seen in the doll with subtle gold highlights in her platinum hair, a soft dimpled mouth, and serene brown eyes that looked wise beyond her doll years? The young woman's cheekbones were soft and rounded, and one eyebrow was ever so slightly higher than the other—like Karin's had been. Sharon nearly gasped at an almost physical stab to her heart. She'd never realized! "That will be $55.82," she said, quickly replacing the lid as her pulse raced.

The girl rambled on. "My Emma calls it her 'guarding angel.' I told her she has one, you know, and that God is taking care of her and—"

"I'm sorry, but it's late, and I have to close," Sharon stammered.

"Yes, of course." The girl pulled the bills from her wallet—three tens and two dollar bills.

"It's $55.82—the balance of your final payment," Sharon stated flatly. "That includes the tax and holding fee."

"But I thought—" The girl looked into her empty wallet again, her fingers trembling. "I don't have that much. I have just the regular $28. I didn't realize—"

Sharon pushed the contract toward her, the one they'd agreed on back in November. She looked at the name: Sarah Schofield. The girl's name was Sarah. "It's right here: "Final payment is $55.82.'"

The silence in the shop hung heavy, and Sharon felt her pulse tapping in her temples. "I'm sorry, Mrs. Schofield. Can't you put it on your credit card, or something, if you don't have the cash?" *Sarah Schofield. They did have names of course, but it was better for all concerned to keep everything completely professional. Wasn't it?*

Sarah's eyes filled with tears. "I don't have a credit card. Mother thought it was best not to get one until I get on my feet financially. Ron isn't coming home from Iraq . . . and what with Emma being—" She stopped and put her hand to her mouth, as though to stop from crying out. Then she seemed to pull herself together. "Well, if I can get the rest of the money I'll be back tonight."

"I'm sorry. I close in 10 minutes." Sharon was surprised at the coldness in her own voice. "You'll have to come back on Monday." She didn't trust herself to look into those tearful green eyes. She never should have entered into this layaway business. A girl with no means, no credit, buying a costly designer doll. It was crazy. She should have known better.

Suddenly Sarah raced out of the shop without another word or look. The bell clanged unmusically after her, and it seemed to Sharon that the air had changed, grown heavy, stifling. She wanted to run too, far away. But where could she escape from the memories, from the sense that all these years she'd been creating dolls to replace the child she had lost? Had she failed with Kevin, too? Failed the little boy who had craved only her love, the gift of herself? Had there been nothing left for him?

When she finally moved to turn out the lights in her shop, an hour had gone by since Sarah Schofield had fled. There would be no gift from the single mother left with a child, a victim of war. No doll for Emma. No guardian angel.

Suddenly, something broke inside her, and before she knew what she was doing, Sharon had scooped up the long white box and the invoice pad, and a piece of her heart she'd forgotten.

It wasn't hard to find 7409 Elm Street. The town of Hadley wasn't very big, and the house was small and rundown, as she'd expected, though, surprisingly, the lit-

tle front porch was tidy, and lights from a small tree—charming in the snow—gleamed in the front window like the Christmas cards she never sent any more.

The door opened almost immediately, and Sarah herself stood there, green eyes alight, not a trace of a tear, only open-mouthed surprise. The strains of "O Come, All Ye Faithful" played softly from a television special, and under the tree lay a miniature crèche with a white-winged angel hovering overhead. "Merry Christmas!" Sarah said shyly.

"It just wouldn't be right to make her wait until Monday," Sharon said briskly, holding the doll out toward Sarah. "Please, give this to your little girl." A strange peace lay lightly on her consciousness, as though she were being introduced to a new world.

"Oh!" Sarah stammered. Th-thank you! I'll have the rest of the money by—"

"Never mind," Sharon said. "The extra twenty or so can be my present."

"Please come and meet my Emma. She'll be so excited. Come!" Sarah tugged at Sharon's hand and drew her into a room off the little hallway where an older woman sat next to a bed with a book in her hand, as though she'd been reading to the little girl who lay there.

"Hello, Emma." Even if she hadn't seen the pale contours of the thin face, the dark shadows beneath the eyes, green like her mother's, Sharon knew that the little girl was not just tucked away for the night at 6:30 on Christmas Eve. The child's shy smile of greeting was too much. Stricken, Sharon ran from the room.

At the sound of footsteps, she turned. The child's

grandmother held out a tentative hand. "Emma's been very sick They've done all they can, but the cancer . . . Well, you know. But the doll has made her so happy."

"Yes, thank you! " Sarah had joined them at the door.

But what strange reality was this? Sharon gazed at the girl who'd lost her husband in Iraq, who cleaned hotel rooms for a pittance, and came home to a child who might not be alive next Christmas. Yet here she stood—joyful, faithful.

More hair had escaped the confines of Sarah's pony-tail and wisped softly around her glowing face. "Mom made gingerbread today. Can you stay for coffee?"

Sharon felt a smile creeping up from some unknown part of her, some part that remembered what it was like to believe, to care even when it hurt. "No. Thank you very much, but I have to get home. I have an important call to make." She couldn't help reaching out to touch Sarah's cheek, but it was Kevin's face she saw. "You will come by the shop again—just to say hello . . ." She paused. "And Merry Christmas!"

Petronella

Temple Bailey

Beautiful Petronella had everything: health, happiness, looks, and money. But she didn't have Justin. The money stood in the way.

Even at Christmas.

So . . . it was all but over.

I f you loved a man and knew that he loved you, and he wouldn't ask you to marry him, what would you do?"

The Admiral surveyed his grand-niece thoughtfully. "What do you expect to do, my dear?"

Petronella stopped on the snowy top step and looked down at him. "Who said I had anything to do with it?" she demanded.

The Admiral's old eyes twinkled. "Let me come in, and tell me about it"

Petronella smiled at him over her big muff. "If you'll promise not to stay after 5:00 I'll give you a cup of tea."

"Who's coming at 5:00?"

The color flamed into Petronella's cheeks. In her white coat and white furs, with her wind-blown brown hair, her beauty satisfied even the Admiral's critical survey, and he hastened to follow his question by the assertion, "Of course I'll come in."

Petronella, with her coat off, showed a slenderness that was enhanced by the straight lines of her white wool gown with long, fur-edged sleeves, and with fur at the top of the high, transparent collar. She wore her hair curled over her ears and low on her forehead, which made of her face a small and delicate oval. In the big hall, with a roaring fire in the wide fireplace, she dispensed comforting hospitality to the adoring Admiral. And when she had given him his tea, she sat on a stool at his feet. "Oh, wise great-uncle," she said, "I am going to tell you about the Man!"

"Have I ever seen him?"

"No. I met him in London last year, and—well, you know what a trip home on shipboard means, with all the women shut up in their cabins, and with moonlight nights, and nobody on deck—"

"So it was an affair of moonlight and propinquity?"

After a pause: "No, it was an affair of the only man in the world for me."

"My dear child!"

Out of a long silence she went on. "He thought I was poor. You know how quietly I traveled with Miss Danvers. And he didn't associate Nell Hewlett with Petronella Hewlett of New York and Great Rock. And so, well, you know, Uncle, he let himself go, and I let myself go, and then—" She drew a long breath. "When we landed, things stopped. He found out who I was, and he wrote me a little note, and said he would never forget our friendship—and that's—all."

She finished drearily, and the bluff old Admiral cleared his throat. There was something wrong with the scheme of things when his Petronella couldn't have the moon if she wanted it!

"And what can I do—what can any woman do?" Petronella demanded, turning on him. "I can't go to him and say, 'Please marry me.' I can't even *think* of it!" Her cheeks burned. "And he'd die before *he'd* say another word, and I suppose that now we'll go on growing old, and I'll get thinner and thinner, and he'll get fatter and fatter, and I'll be an old maid, and he'll marry some woman who's poor enough to satisfy his pride, and, well, that will be the end of it, Uncle."

"The end of it?" said the gentleman who had once commanded a squadron. "Well, I guess not, Petronella, if you want him. Oh, the man's a fool!"

"He's not a fool, Uncle." The sparks in Petronella's eyes matched the sparks in the Admiral's.

"Well, if he's worthy of you—"

Petronella laid her cheek against his hand. "The question is not of his worthiness," she said faintly, "but of mine, dear uncle."

Dumbly, the Admiral gazed down at that drooping head. Could this be Petronella—confident, imperious, the daughter of a confident and imperious race?

He took refuge in the question, "But who is coming at 5:00?"

"*He* is coming. He is passing through Boston on his way to visit his mother in Maine. I asked him to come. I told him I was down here by the sea, and intended to spend Christmas at Great Rock because you were here, and because this was the house I lived in when I was a little girl, and that I wanted him to see it; and—I told him the truth, Uncle."

"The truth?"

"That I missed him. That was all I dared say, and I wish you had read his note of assent. Such a stiff little thing. It threw me back upon myself, and I wished I hadn't written him—I wished he wouldn't come. Oh, Uncle, if I were a man I'd give a woman the right to choose. That's the reason there are so many unhappy marriages. Nine wrong men ask a woman, and the tenth right one *won't*. And finally she gets tired of waiting for the tenth right one, and marries one of the nine wrong ones."

"There are women today," said the Admiral, "who are preaching a woman's right to propose."

Petronella gazed at him thoughtfully. "I could preach a doctrine like that—but I couldn't practice it. It's easy enough to say to some other woman, 'Ask him,' but it's different when you are the woman."

"Yet if he asked you," suggested the Admiral, "the world might say that he wanted your money."

"Why should we care what the world would say?" Petronella was on her feet now, defending her cause vigorously. "Why should we care? Why, it's our love against the world, Uncle! Why should we care?"

The Admiral stood up, too, and paced the rug as in former days he had paced the decks of his ship. "There must be some way out," he said at last, and stopped short. "Suppose I speak to him—"

"And spoil it all? Oh, Uncle!" Petronella shook him by the lapels of his blue coat. "A man never knows how a woman feels about such things. Even you don't, you old darling. And now will you please go; and take this because I love you"—and she kissed him on one cheek—"and this because it is a quarter to five, and you'll have to

hurry"—and she kissed him on the other cheek.

The Admiral, being helped into his big cape in the hall, called back, "I forgot to give you your Christmas present," and he produced a small package.

"Come here and let me open it," Petronella insisted.

And the Admiral, without a glance at the accusing clock, went back. And thus it happened that he was there to meet the Man.

It must be confessed that the Admiral suffered a distinct shock as he was presented to the hero of Petronella's romance. Here was no courtly youth of the type of the military male line of Petronella's family, but a muscular young giant of masterful bearing. The Hewlett men had commanded men, and one could see at a glance that Justin Hare had also commanded women. This, the wise old Admiral decided at once, was the thing that had attracted Petronella— Petronella, who had held her own against all masculine encroachments, and who was heart-free at 25!

"Look what this dearest dear of an uncle has given me," said Petronella, and held up for the young surgeon's admiration a string of pearls with a sapphire clasp. "They belonged to my great-aunt. I was named for her, and Uncle says I look like her."

"You have her eyes, my dear, and some of her ways. But she was less independent. In her time, women leaned more, as it were, on man's strength."

Justin Hare looked at them with interest—at the slender girl in her white gown; at the tall, straight old man with his air of command.

"Women in these days do not lean," he said with decision. "They lead."

A spark came into Petronella's eyes. "And do you like the modern type best?" she challenged.

He answered with smiling directness, "I like you."

The Admiral was pleased with that, though he was still troubled by this man's difference from the men of his own race. Yet if back of that honest bluntness there was a heart that would enshrine her, well, that was all he would ask for this dearest of girls.

He glanced at the clock, and spoke hurriedly: "I must be going, my dear; it is long after 5:00."

"Must you really go?" asked the mendacious Petronella.

An hour later she was alone. The visit had been a failure. She admitted that, as she gazed with a sort of agonized dismay through the wide window to where the sea was churned by the wildness of the northeast gale. Snow had come with the wind, shutting out the view of the great empty hotels on the Point, shutting out, too, the golden star of hope which gleamed from the top of the lighthouse.

Petronella turned away from the blank scene with a little shudder. Thus had Justin Hare shut her out of his life. He had talked of his mother in Maine, of his hospital plans for the winter, but not a word had he said of those moonlit nights when he had masterfully swayed her by the force of his own passion, had wooed her, won her.

And now there was nothing that she could do. There was never anything that a woman could do! And so she must bear it. Oh, if she *could* bear it!

A little later, when a maid slipped in to light the candles, Petronella said out of the shadows, "When Jenkins goes to the post office, I have a parcel for the mail."

"He's been, miss, and there won't be any train out tonight; the snow has stopped the trains."

Not any train! At first the remark held little significance, but finally the fact beat against her brain. If the one evening train could not leave, then Justin Hare must stay in town, and he would have to stay until Christmas morning!

Petronella went at once to the telephone and called up the only hotel that was open at that season. Presently she had Hare on the other end of the line.

"You must come to my house to dinner," she said. "Jenkins has told me about your train. Please don't dress up—there'll be only Miss Danvers and Uncle; and you shall help me trim my little tree."

Although she told him not to change clothes, she changed her gown for one of dull green velvet, built on the simple lines of the white wool she had worn in the afternoon. The square neck was framed by a collar of Venetian point, and there was a queer old pin of pearls.

The Admiral, arriving early, demanded, "My dear, what is this? I was just sitting down to bread and milk and a handful of raisins, and now I must dine in six courses, and drink coffee, which will keep me awake!"

She laid her cheek against his arm. "Mr. Hare's train couldn't get out of town on account of the snow."

"And he's coming?"

"Yes."

"But, what about this afternoon, my dear?"

She slipped her hand into his, and they stood gazing into the fire. "It was dreadful, Uncle. I had a feeling that I had compelled him to come—against his will."

"Yet you have asked him to come again tonight?"

She shivered a little, and her hand was cold. "Perhaps I shall regret it, but oh, Uncle, can't I have for this one evening the joy of his presence? And if tomorrow my heart dies—"

"Nella, my dear child!"

The Admiral's own Petronella had never drawn in this way upon his emotions. She had been gentle, perhaps a little cold. But then he had always worshipped at her shrine. Perhaps a woman denied the love she yearns for learns the value of it. At any rate, here in his arms was the dearest thing in his lonely life, sobbing as if her heart would break.

When Justin came a half-hour later he found them still in front of the fire in the great hall, and as she rose to welcome him he saw that Petronella had been sitting on a stool at her uncle's feet.

Hare took a chair on the hearth, and she chose another with a high, carved back, in which she sat with her silken ankles crossed and the tips of her slipper toes resting on a leopard-skin that the Admiral had brought back from India.

"When I was a little girl," she explained, "we always spent Christmas Eve in this house by the sea instead of in town. We were all here then—Mother and Dad and dear Aunt Pet—and we hung our stockings at this very fireplace. And now there is no one but Miss Danvers and me, and Uncle, who lives up aloft in his big house across the way, where he has a lookout tower. I always feel like calling up to him when I go there, 'Oh, Anne, Sister Anne, do you see anybody coming?'"

She was talking nervously, with her cheeks as white as a lily, but with her eyes smiling. The Admiral glanced at Hare. The young man was drinking in her beauty. But suddenly he frowned and turned away his eyes.

"It was very good of you to ask me over," he said, formally.

That steadied Petronella. Her nervous self-consciousness fled, and she was at once the gracious, impersonal hostess.

The Admiral glowed with pride of her. *She'll carry it off*, he said to himself. *It's in her blood.*

"Dinner is served," announced Jenkins from the doorway, and then Miss Danvers came down and greeted Justin, and they all went out together.

There was holly for a centerpiece, and four red candles in silver holders. The table was of richly carved mahogany, and the Admiral, following an old custom, served the soup from a silver tureen, upheld by four fat cupids. From the wide arch that led into the great hall was hung a bunch of mistletoe. Beyond the arch the roaring fire made a background of gleaming, golden light.

To the young surgeon it seemed a fairy scene flaming with the color and glow of a life that he had never known. He had lived so long surrounded by the bare, blank walls of a hospital. Even Petronella's soft green gown seemed made of some mystical stuff that had nothing in common with the cool white or blue starchiness of the uniforms of nurses.

They talked of many things, covering with their commonplaces the tenseness of the situation. Then suddenly the conversation took a significant turn.

"I love these stormy nights," Petronella said, "with the snow blowing, and the wind, and the house all warm and bright."

"Think of the poor sailors at sea," Hare reminded her.

"Please. I don't want to think of them. We have done our best for them, Uncle and I. We have opened a reading room down by the docks, so that all who are ashore can have soup and coffee and sandwiches, and there's a big stove, and newspapers and magazines."

"You dispense charity?"

"Why not?" she asked him confidently. "We have plenty—why shouldn't we give?"

"Because it takes away from their manhood to receive."

The Admiral spoke bluntly. "The men don't feel that way. This charity, as you call it, is a memorial to my wife. The grandfathers of these boys used to see her light in the window of the old house on stormy nights, and they knew that it was an invitation to good cheer. More than one crew coming in half frozen was glad of the soup and coffee that were sent down to them in cans with baskets of bread. And this little coffee room has been the outgrowth of just such hospitality. There are too many of the men to have in my house; I simply entertain them elsewhere, and I like to go and talk to them, and sometimes Petronella goes."

"There's a picture of dear Aunt Pet hanging there," said Petronella, "and you can't imagine how it softens the manners of the men. It is as if her spirit brooded over the place. They have made it into a sort of shrine, and they bring shells and queer carved things to put on the shelf below it."

"In the city we're beginning to think that such methods weaken self-respect."

"That's because in the city there isn't any real democracy," said the wise old Admiral. "You give your friend a cup of coffee and think nothing of it, yet when I give a cup of coffee to a sailor whose grandfather and mine fished together on the banks, you warn me that my methods tend to pauperize. In the city the poor are never your friends—in this little town no man would admit that he is less than I. They like my coffee, and they drink it."

Petronella, seeing her chance, took it. "I think people are horrid to let money make a difference."

"You say that," said Hare, "because you've never had to accept favors. You have, in other words, never been on the other side."

The Admiral, taking up cudgels for his niece, answered, "If she had been on the other side, she would have taken life as she takes it now—like a gentleman and a soldier," and he smiled at Petronella.

Hare had a baffled sense that the Admiral was right, that Petronella's fineness and delicacy would never go down in defeat or despair. She would hold her head high though the heavens fell. But could any man make such demands upon her? For himself, he would not.

So he answered doggedly, "We shall hope she need never be tested." And Petronella's heart sank like lead.

But presently she began to talk about the little tree. "We have always had it in Uncle's lookout tower. That was another of dear Aunt Pet's thoughts for the sailors. On clear nights they looked through their binoculars for the little colored lights, and on stormy nights they knew that back of all the snow was that Christmas brightness."

"I never had a tree," said Justin. "When I was a kid

we had pretty hard times, and the best Christmas I remember was one when Mother made us boys put up a shelf for our books, and she started our collection with *Treasure Island* and *Huckleberry Finn.*"

In the adjoining room volumes reached from floor to ceiling, from end to end. Petronella had a vision of this vivid young giant gloating over his two books on a rude shelf. And all her life she had had the things she wanted! Somehow the thought took the bitterness out of her attitude toward him. How strong he must be to deny himself now the one great thing that he craved when his life had held so little.

"How lovely to begin with just those two books," she said, softly, and the radiance of her smile was dazzling.

When she showed him her presents she was still radiant. There was an opera bag of Chinese needlework and handles of jade, a Damascus bowl of pierced brass, and a tea caddy in quaint Dutch *repoussé*. There was a silver-embroidered altar cloth for a cushion and a bit of Copenhagen faience, all the sophisticated artistry which is sent to those who have no need for the commonplace. There were jewels, too: a bracelet of topazes surrounded by brilliants, a pair of slipper buckles of turquoises set in silver, a sapphire circlet for her little finger, a pendant of seed pearls.

As she opened the parcels and displayed her riches Justin felt bewildered. His gifts to his mother had usually included gloves and a generous check. If he had ventured to choose anything for Petronella he would not have dared go beyond a box of candy or a book. He had given his nurses handbags and handkerchiefs. And the men of Petronella's world bestowed on her brass bowls and tea caddies!

Miss Danvers vanished upstairs. The Admiral, having admired, slipped away to the library, encouraged by Petronella's whispered "Oh, Uncle dear, leave us alone for just a little minute. I've found a way!"

Then Petronella, with that radiance still upon her, sat down on her little stool in front of the fire and looked at Justin on the other side of the hearth. "You haven't given me anything," she began, reproachfully.

"What could I give that would compare with these?" His hand swept toward the exquisite display. "What could I give—"

"There's one thing," she said softly.

"What?"

"That copy of *Treasure Island* that your mother gave you long ago."

Dead silence. Then, unsteadily, "Why should you want *that?*"

"Because your mother—loved you."

Again, dead silence. Hare did not look at her. His hand clenched the arm of his chair. His face was white. Then, very low, "Why do you make it hard for me?"

"Because I want the book." She was smiling at him with her eyes like stars. "I want to read it with the eyes of the little boy—With the eyes of the little boy who looked into the future and saw life as a great adventure, who looked into the future—and dreamed."

He had a vision, too, of that little boy, reading, in the old house in the Maine woods, by the light of an oil lamp on Christmas Eve, with the snow blowing outside as it blew tonight.

44

"And your mother loved you because she loved your father," the girl's voice went on, "and you were all very happy up there in the forest. Do you remember that you told me about it on the ship? You were happy, although you were poor and hadn't any books but *Treasure Island* and *Huckleberry Finn*. But your mother was happy—because she loved your father."

As she repeated it she leaned forward. "Could you think of your mother as having been happy with any one else but your father?" she asked. "Could you think of her as having never married him, of having gone through the rest of her days a half-woman, because he would not take her into his life? Can you think that all the money in the world—all the money in the whole world—would have made up—"

The room seemed to darken. Hare was conscious that her face was hidden in her hands, that he stumbled toward her, that he knelt beside her—that she was in his arms. "Hush," he was saying in that beating darkness of emotion. "Hush, don't cry! I—I will never let you go!"

* * *

When the storm had spent itself, and when at last she met his long gaze, he whispered, "I'm not even sure now that it is right."

"You *will* be sure as the years go on," she whispered back; then, tremulously, "but I—I could never have talked that way if I had thought of you as the man. I had to think of you as the little boy who dreamed."

A Song for Elizabeth

Robin Cole

Elizabeth was old and senile, and nobody at the convalescent home seemed to know what to do with her. If only she wouldn't keep repeating those two ridiculous words, "Doop doop," again and again! And nobody knew what they meant to her.

Then Christmas came once again.

December snow swept across the parking lot of Crescent Manor Convalescent Home. As the youngest nurse on the staff, I sat with the charge nurse at the North Wing station, staring out the double-glass doors and waiting for the first wave of evening visitors. At the sound of bedroom slippers flapping against bare heels, I turned to see Elizabeth, one of our patients, striding down the corridor.

"Oh, please," groaned the charge nurse, "not tonight! Not when we're shorthanded already!"

Rounding the corner, Elizabeth jerked the sash of her tired chenille robe tighter around her skinny waist. We hadn't combed her hair for a while, and it made a scraggly halo around her wrinkled face.

"Doop doop," she said, nodding quickly and hurrying on. "Doop doop," she said to the man in the day room, slumped in front of the TV, a belt holding him in his wheelchair.

The charge nurse turned to me. "Can you settle her down?"

"Shall I go after her, or wait till she comes around again?"

"Just wait. I may need you here before she gets back. She never does any harm. It's just that ridiculous sound she makes. I wonder if she thinks she's saying words."

A group of visitors swept through the front doors, scraping feet on the rug, shaking snow from their coats, cleaning their glasses. They clustered around the desk, seeking information, and as they did Elizabeth came striding by again. "Doop doop," she said happily to everyone. I moved out to intercept the purposeful strider.

"Elizabeth," I said, taking her bony elbow, "I need you to do something for me. Come and sit down and I'll tell you about it." I was stalling. This wasn't anything I had learned in training, but I would think of *something*.

The charge nurse stared at me, shaking her head, then turned her attention to the group of visitors surrounding the desk. Nobody ever got Elizabeth to do anything. We counted it a good day if we could keep her from pacing the halls.

Elizabeth stopped. She looked into my face with a puzzled frown. "Doop doop," she said.

I led her to a writing table in the day room and

46

found a piece of paper and a pencil.

"Sit down here at the desk, Elizabeth. Write your name for me."

Her watery eyes grew cloudy. Deep furrows appeared between her brows. She took the stubby pencil in her gnarled hand and held it above the paper. Again and again, she looked at the paper then at me, questioningly.

"Here. I'll write it first, and then you can copy it, OK?"

In large, clear script, I wrote, *Elizabeth Goode*. "There you are. You stay here and copy that. I'll be right back."

At the door of the day room I turned, half expecting to see her following me, but she sat quietly, pencil in hand. The only sound now came from the muffled voices of visitors and their ailing loved ones.

"Elizabeth is writing," I told the charge nurse. I could hardly believe it.

"Fantastic," she said calmly. "You'd better not leave her alone for long. We don't have time to clean pencil marks off the walls tonight." She turned away, avoiding my eyes. "Oh, I almost forgot—Novak and Sellers both have that rotten flu. They'll be out all week. Looks like you'll be working Christmas Eve." She pulled a metal-backed chart from the file and was suddenly very busy.

I swallowed hard. Until now I had loved my independence, my own small trailer. At 22 I was just out of nurse's training and on my own.

But I had never spent Christmas Eve away from my parents and my brothers. That wasn't in the picture at all when I moved away from home—I planned to go home for holidays.

Words raced through my head: *They'll go to the candlelight service without me! They'll read the stories, and I won't be there to hear! What kind of Christmas can I have in a little trailer with nothing to decorate but a potted fern? How can it be Christmas if I can't be the first one up to turn on the tree lights? Who'll make the cocoa for the family?*

Tears burned my eyes, but I blinked them back. Nodding slowly, I walked toward the day room.

Elizabeth sat at the writing table, staring down at the paper in front of her. Softly, I touched my hand to her fragile shoulder, and she looked up with a smile. She handed me the paper. Under my big, bold writing was a wobbly signature. *Elizabeth Goode*, it read.

"Doop doop," said Elizabeth with satisfaction.

Later that night, when all the visitors were gone and the North Wing was dark and silent, I sat with the charge nurse, completing charts. "Do you suppose I could take Elizabeth out tomorrow?" I asked. In good weather, we often took the patients for walks or rides, but I didn't know about snowy nights. "I'd like to go to Christmas Eve service, and I think she'd like to go with me."

"Wouldn't she be a problem? What about the *doop doop?*"

"I think I can explain it to her. You know, nobody else talks during church, so she'd probably be quiet too. Look how well she did this afternoon when I

gave her something to do."

The charge nurse looked thoughtful. "Things would be a lot easier around here if you did take her. Then you could get her ready for bed when you got back. There'll be visitors to help with the others, but nobody has been here for Elizabeth in a long time. I'll ask her doctor for you."

* * *

And so it was that a first-year nurse and a tall, skinny old woman arrived at First Church on Christmas Eve just before the service began. The snow had stopped, and the stars were brilliant in the clear, cold sky.

"Now, Elizabeth," I said, "I don't know how much you can understand, but listen to me. We're going in to sit down with the rest of the people. There'll be music and someone will read. There'll be kids in costumes, too. But we aren't going to say anything. We'll stand up when it's time to sing, and we'll hold the hymnal together."

Elizabeth looked grave. "Doop doop," she said.

Oh, Lord, I hope she understands! I thought. *Suppose she gets up and heads down the aisle wishing everyone a doop doop?*

I wrapped Elizabeth's coat and shawl around her and tucked my arm under hers. Together we entered the candlelit church. Elizabeth's watery old eyes gleamed, and her face crinkled in a smile. But she said nothing.

The choir entered singing. The pastor read the Christmas story from the Bible: "And there were in the same country, shepherds . . ."

Costumed children took their places at the front of the church: shepherds and wise men, angels and the holy family. Elizabeth watched, but she said nothing. The congregation rose to sing "Joy to the World." Elizabeth stood, holding the hymnal with me, her mouth closed. The lights in the sanctuary dimmed, and two white-robed angels lit the candelabra. Finally the organ began the introduction to "Silent Night," and we stood again.

I handed the hymnal to Elizabeth but she shook her head. A cold dread gathered at the back of my neck. Now what? Would this be the moment when she started wandering down the aisle? I looked at her wrinkled face out of the corner of my eye, trying to guess her thoughts. The singing began. I sang as loudly as I could, hoping to attract Elizabeth's attention. As I paused for breath, I heard a thin, cracked voice.

"Sleep in heavenly peace," it sang. "Sleep in heavenly peace."

Elizabeth! Staring straight ahead, candlelight reflected in her eyes, she was singing the words without consulting the hymnal.

O Lord, forgive me, I prayed. *Sometimes I forget. Of course it can be Christmas with only a fern to decorate. Of course it can be Christmas without a tree or the family or cocoa. Christmas is the story of love. It's the birth of the Son of God, and it can live in the heart and memory of a gray-haired old woman.*

"Christ the Savior is born," sang Elizabeth. "Christ the Savior is born."

"Merry Christmas, Elizabeth," I whispered, gently patting her arm.

"Doop doop," Elizabeth replied contentedly.

Flocks By Night

Bruce Douglas

John Farrell was first into the valley. Now he ruled its cattle ranches as a king. No one came in without his blessing.

Then, at the far end of the valley, came a foreign family, who dared to bring in sheep. That meant war.

And the coming blizzard made no difference . . .

When a man is the first White man to settle in a virgin valley, that man, if he be thoughtful and foresighted, is likely to be concerned about the families that move in after him and settle down to be his neighbors. He is apt to feel that it is his own personal business who comes in—and to make it his business. And as the years go by and he becomes a cattle king and the original log house that he built is now just a storage shed out behind the big ranch house, he is apt to take on the stature of a patriarch.

John Farrell was like that. Silver Creek Valley was his valley, his because he got there first and made it his. He coddled it, cared for it, watched over it, and bossed and bullied it like the benevolent old despot he was. The neighbors who settled in Silver Creek Valley were folks of whom he approved. And if he did not approve of any settler, John Farrell made it plenty hard for that man to stay.

"A man has got to neighbor with them that settle," John Farrell would say, "and his children with their children, and his grandchildren with their grandchildren. We've got to be careful who we let stay."

* * *

When John Farrell brought his wife and infant son into Silver Creek Valley, it wasn't until the second summer that he got his house finished and the family moved in. It was a sturdy, weather-tight house, with puncheon floor, log walls well-notched and quartered, a tight roof of shakes to make it dry from rain and snow, and a wide stone fireplace to keep it warm. But it was an enduring hard task for one man working alone, and the first blizzard caught him with his walls not yet finished and the roof not yet on. So the Farrells shivered through their first winter in a pole lean-to thatched with pine boughs, backed up against a granite cliff.

When Ben and Florence Cullum moved into the valley, after Ben Cullum had got his floor and chimney built and his logs shaped (and after John Farrell had looked the Cullums over aplenty and approved them), Farrell pitched in with Cullum to raise the house. So the Cullums were settled in their home by first frost. A year later, Farrell and Cullum pitched in to help raise Frank Sutton's house. And by the time John Farrell's boy, Tom, grew up and married Ben Cullum's daughter, Ann, who was the first White child born in Silver Creek Valley, there were enough cattlemen and cowboys in the valley so that a house raising had become a matter of five or six hours' work, with a barbecue to follow. And it had become a kind of symbol, welcoming a neighbor to permanence in the valley.

* * *

Then Pieter Ashjian, with his wife Hilda and their 2-year-old son, Little Piet, moved in one spring, taking up a claim at the extreme south end of the valley. Though Pieter Ashjian had his floor and chimney built by fall, and his logs notched and quartered and his shakes split, not one hand was lifted in Silver Creek Valley to help him raise his house.

There were several reasons. In the first place, Pieter Ashjian was primarily a sodbuster and only brought in some cattle after he had got 40 acres under plow and fence. And sodbusters are none too welcome in a cattlemen's valley.

Too, they were foreigners, and hence subject to strong suspicion. Hilda Ashjian was either German or Dutch, a placid blue-eyed, yellow-haired woman of mild speech and manners, and with a pleasant, slow smile whenever she was given opportunity to show it. Pieter Ashjian was vaguely classified as from one of those Central or Southern European countries, no one knew which, nor cared enough to ask. He was a short, stocky, weather-tanned man, with a barrel chest and heavily-muscled arms and legs. His hair was black over a broad forehead and dark eyes that were calm and wide apart.

"Them foreigners," John Farrell said (and when John Farrell spoke he voiced the thought of Silver Creek Valley) "are a shiftless, gypsy sort. They don't have staying quality. They ain't permanent and don't know what real responsibility means. Come a few hardships, and

they move on. Leave this family alone, and they won't last out a year in Silver Creek Valley. You'll see."

So Silver Creek Valley left the Ashjians strictly alone and sat back and watched from a distance. They watched while Pieter Ashjian fashioned himself a wooden plow, a plow as rude as Pieter's ancestors must have used a thousand years before somewhere along the Danube. They watched him plow his field and commented on how this man was not even putting up a pole shelter but was making his family live in their Conestoga wagon while he broke the sod. Some put it down as evidence of the shiftless gypsy ways that John Farrell had foretold.

But soon they found out why Pieter Ashjian plowed first before building. For instead of raising a shelter out of poles and brush, he took the sod from the furrows he had cut and reared a sod house. That was something new and strange in Silver Creek Valley, emphasizing the fact that Pieter Ashjian was a foreigner. For with all the enclosing mountain slopes covered with pine, folks looked to the trees and brush for materials for shelter and to the sod only for food for their cattle. Yet they had to admit among themselves, the sod hut was stouter than a pole lean-to, though it leaked smoke through every opening when Hilda Ashjian was cooking.

They sat back and watched all through the summer while Pieter Ashjian raised a good field crop of wheat, and a mixed garden patch close to the little sod hut. In all the spare hours between dawn and dark he cut trees on the mountainside, shaped his logs, and snaked them down to where his log house was to be. They watched him move big boulders from the stream bed and build a

wide fireplace and chimney. And they watched him lay his puncheon floor and smooth it down and get his first rows of log wall laid.

* * *

But in the fall, after Pieter Ashjian had sold his crop and bought a new plow and fence wire and other necessities, disturbing rumors spread through Silver Creek Valley. Besides fencing his plowed land separately, Pieter Ashjian was fencing his whole claim, running his poles for more than a mile, clear across the south end of the valley, from slope to slope.

This was not disquieting in itself—there were others in Silver Creek Valley who had fenced their whole claims. Gus Whately, for example, who was raising purebred Herefords and didn't want them to get their strains mixed on the open range. The disquieting thing was the kind of fence that Pieter Ashjian was stringing. It was a four-strand fence instead of a two or a three. And the bottom wires were strung close together, with a wide space between the third and the top, as though the bottom three strands were calculated to hold in smaller animals than steers.

Ben Cullum and Frank Sutton rode over personally to talk it over with John Farrell.

"It wouldn't be sheep?" Ben Cullum ventured.

Frank Sutton said, "If it was sheep he wouldn't need that top strand of wire."

Cullum nodded. "But," he puzzled, "if it's cattle, he's wasted a mile, mebbe two mile, of wire making that bottom so tight. I've watched the man, an' he don't look like a waster."

Frank Sutton spoke grimly. "Silver Creek Valley is cattle. If that *@#! foreigner tries to run stinkin' woollies . . ."

They both looked questioningly at old John Farrell. But John Farrell merely shook his gray head and, through lips slightly tense, said: "Wait."

They waited. And when Pieter Ashjian turned three cows, five steers and a bull into his fenced grazing land about the time the first light frost hit Silver Creek Valley, the tension eased off. Frank Sutton brought the news over from his Slash-S, making a special trip for the purpose.

"It's cattle," he declared. "So whatever them extra bottom strands of wire are for, it can't be sheep, 'cause cattle and sheep won't graze together. A self-respectin' steer will starve before he'll eat where sheep graze. Sort o' glad it come out this way. That hombre's done about as well as any of us did in his first year. Wouldn't like to have to run him out account o' sheep."

But the relief was short-lived. One week later a rider came larruping over from the Slash-S and reported to John Farrell that there were a score, or more, sheep in Ashjian's grazing land, right along with the cattle.

John Farrell's faded blue eyes grew bleak. He gave orders. And that evening at sundown a committee of valley ranchers rode grimly along the backbone of the valley and up to Pieter Ashjian's sod hut.

Pieter Ashjian appeared in the doorway. His calm, dark eyes lighted at first sight of the riders, but grew cloudy as he took in their grim looks and the rifles and belt-guns they bore. He stepped quickly back into the hut. When he came out again a new double-barreled shotgun hung in the crook of his arm. Behind him Little Piet thrust a chubby face around the corner of the door, peering questioningly, before he was hurriedly snatched back inside.

The homesteader waited in grave silence, and for a time there were no sounds save the creaking of saddles and the stamp of a restless horse. Then John Farrell spoke. The gray old warrior sat straight as a ramrod in his saddle, his blue eyes staring bleakly down at Pieter Ashjian from beneath bushy brows that were tipped with snow. John Farrell could keep an open mind, even about a foreigner. He could wait and watch to find out whether Pieter Ashjian was a shiftless, gypsy sort, or a man of permanence and responsibility. But on the matter of sheep, John Farrell's mind had been made up for more than 30 years.

"Pieter Ashjian," he said, "you have brought sheep into Silver Creek Valley. This is a cattle valley. The sheep must go."

Just that, and no more. The edict of a king. To be backed up by force if necessary. Silence fell again, and Pieter Ashjian met the old cattleman's gaze unwaveringly, standing squarely in front of his doorway, his feet braced slightly apart. When he spoke, there was a foreign accent, and he chose his words slowly.

"This is America. I am an American; I have taken out my papers. In America a man does what he chooses with his own. My sheep will stay on my own land. Now get off my place!"

Behind John Farrell the voice of Frank Sutton rose in angry impatience. "Silver Creek Valley is cattle. No *@#! foreigner is goin' to foul this valley with stinkin' woolies!"

Pieter Ashjian flushed darkly, and John Farrell silenced Frank Sutton with a gesture. He spoke calmly, persuasively. "You don't understand, bein' a foreigner. You've put sheep and cattle together in your fenced grazing. But sheep and cattle don't mix. Sheep ruin grazing land for cattle, because cattle won't graze where sheep graze. You'll find that out; and to save your cattle you'll turn your sheep out onto the public range. We can't have that. We've got to stop it before it starts."

Frank Sutton growled again, and muttered something about if they sat there palavering much longer it would be too dark to shoot the stinkin' woolies and have it over with. John Farrell turned an imperious glance his way. And suddenly, surprisingly, Pieter Ashjian was no longer glowering—he was smiling a smile that spread widely over his face and shone in his dark eyes.

"Why!" he exclaimed, as though voicing a sudden discovery, "You fellows ain't bad men! You're just doing what you think you got to. But it ain't so. Look!" He leaned the shotgun against the side of the sod hut, took a dozen steps, and pointed. "You say they don't eat together? Look—over in that fence corner. Even under the cattle's bellies the sheep eat!"

He turned back toward them, and he was shaking his head slowly from side to side, commiserating with them. "You fellows!" he said. "Back in the old country you would have a lot to learn!"

John Farrell led his committee of valley ranchers away from Pieter Ashjian's claim, leaving behind a stern warning to Ashjian to keep his fences tight.

54

But though the old cattleman again commanded watching and waiting, the tension was greater in the valley, and many waited less on Ashjian than on John Farrell, wondering when he would make up his mind to give the word to run the squatter out. Toward Pieter Ashjian they were now openly hostile, for he was now not only a foreigner and a sodbuster but a sheep herder. A sheepherder in a cattlemen's valley. . . .

* * *

And so it was that though Pieter Ashjian had his floor and chimney built, and his logs notched and quartered and his shakes split, not one hand was lifted in Silver Creek Valley to help him raise his house.

He worked alone, taking what time he could from his fall plowing. And day by day and week by week, the log wall grew gradually higher. And then he had his window frames finished and the glass in. But as the walls rose, hoisting each log into its higher place became a more difficult task for a man working alone, and the work progressed more slowly with each passing day. And when the big blizzard pounced down on Silver Creek Valley the day before Christmas, riding a 40-mile-an-hour wind that came howling straight from the North Pole, the walls were not yet finished and the roof not yet on.

The day had dawned clear, with no hint of the blizzard to come. Soon after breakfast the Cullums and the Whatelys and the Suttons had come over to the big Farrell ranch house to help get ready for the Christmas Eve party. And as the morning wore on, other valley families and a scattering of cowboys drifted in. Ever since John Farrell had built a ranch house with a front room big enough to hold everybody, a valley party had been a tradition, with a great Christmas tree in one corner of the room, and a live Santa Claus to take presents off it and hand them to the valley children.

As folks drifted in, Mary Farrell put them to work. There was corn to be popped and strung for the Christmas tree, cooking to be done, and toys to be wrapped and labeled with children's names and hung on the tree.

Shortly before noon, Mary Farrell drew her husband aside from the crowd and spoke to him privately.

"John," she said, her serious brown eyes lifting to his, "shouldn't we lay aside strife just for one night? That family in that tiny sod hut. . . . And there is a child."

John Farrell shook his head impatiently. "No one would have them," he stated flatly. "You don't understand—no one would neighbor with them. They're not permanent, responsible folks like the rest of us. Leave them alone and they'll pull out before spring. You'll see."

Mary Farrell made one more attempt. "But the child. It is hard on a child, at Christmas, John."

She knew before she got the words out that she had failed. John Farrell's blue eyes were frigid. He said, "Our child spent his first Christmas in Silver Creek Valley in a pole lean-to. His only toys were a bean bag you made and four wooden soldiers I whittled from a stick." He walked away from her and looked out a window. Then he turned. "Black clouds piling up in the north," he announced. "Blizzard coming! Tell all the men."

The blizzard struck before the men were all in their saddles, and they started out, some 20 of them, with it howling at their backs and the air suddenly white and thick around them. John Farrell issued commands.

"The cattle can shelter on the slopes under the trees," he shouted, making his voice heard above the shrieking wind. "They'll last it out all right, even if it snows for days. Later we can sort 'em out and bring 'em in for hay feeding. They'll be drifting with the wind. Spread out across the valley and ride south, and whenever you find a bunch of steers, push 'em to the nearest slope."

"South," Frank Sutton's complaining bellow arose. "They'll drift straight south. And if it wasn't for that *#@! sheepherder's fence they'd drift straight on to safety in the trees at the head of the valley!"

All afternoon they worked, in the dull light of a lowering sky, blinded and choked by the solid mass of flakes that raced by them from the north. By 4:00 the wind was slackening a little, the temperature was dropping fast, and the flakes had become small and hard like pellets of corn meal, stinging their reddened cheeks and chapped hands. A dozen times they had come upon bands of steers, heads down, tails to the wind, and pushed them over to whichever slope was nearest. And by 4:00 they had covered all but the south quarter of the valley.

"All the rest will have reached the fence by now," John Farrell decided. "We'll head straight there and pick 'em up."

They pressed on to the fence but found no cattle. Ben Cullum's astonished shout announced the fact. And as they all gathered at the fence, they found signs of trampling beneath the newest drifting of snow, but not a steer in sight. Then suddenly Frank Sutton let out a yell.

"Here comes a bunch, driftin' sideways to the wind! Never heard tell of cattle showin' that much sense before!"

The steers loomed up in the gray dusk, indistinct figures in the wind-driven snow, a bunch of 20 or more. Then at their rear appeared a man on horseback. Faintly, they heard him halloo at the steers as he approached. Then, seeing them, the rider reigned in and turned the collar of his sheepskin jacket back from a reddened face.

Frank Sutton gasped, "It's— Why–why it's that Ashjian feller!"

Pieter Ashjian wiped moisture from his wind-reddened eyes and grinned at the group. "Bad weather, ain't it? She come up quick."

John Farrell pushed his horse out in front of the group, reining in close to the homesteader. "How come you to be pushing these steers, Ashjian?"

Pieter Ashjian shrugged wearily. "In a blizzard cattle drift with the wind until they reach shelter. Unless they get stopped. But my fence stopped 'em. So I got to push 'em along the fence to the trees."

Hard, grain-like snow sifted in beneath John Farrell's collar, lodging at his shoulder blades and sending a shiver through him. It came to him suddenly that the temperature had dropped 20 degrees since noon and was still plummeting. He spoke gravely. "That was a right neighborly act on your part, Ashjian. We'll take over the steers now; and I'd advise you to head for cover and warmth. It's almost dark, and these blizzards can fool you. A man can get frosted before he knows it and lose a leg or an arm if the frost bites too deep."

Peter Ashjian nodded. "I got some things to do first. Then I go home."

They pushed the bunch up into the trees on the west slope. On the way back north they stopped at young Tom Farrell's house while Tom brewed coffee and they warmed the chill out of their bones. Then Tom piled logs in the fireplace so that the house would still be warm when he and Ann and the children returned from his father's house after midnight.

When they started out again, the blizzard was slackening and the cold was intense. It was 6:00, and black darkness had shrouded the valley for two hours by the time they reached the big ranch house.

Mary Farrell hurried out to meet them and stood in the rectangle of light from the door, looking anxiously up at her husband.

"John," she said, "there's trouble. Bad trouble, I'm afraid. Mrs. Ashjian got here just a few minutes ago. She says her husband has been out since noon. An hour after darkness had fallen his horse came back without him. She mounted and tried to back-track, but the blizzard had blotted out the tracks. Then she rode over to ask us to send out a search party."

She fell silent for a moment, showing her concern only in her eyes. But when she spoke next there was a note of defiance in her voice. "She brought the child with her, of course; and I am keeping them here for the party. When you find her husband, bring him here, John."

John Farrell merely nodded, his mind already racing to the task ahead. He sent men to the bunkhouse for lanterns and, when they were lit and hung on saddle horns, led the way southward once again along the center of the valley.

* * *

Finding Pieter Ashjian turned out to be no difficult task, though all were oppressed by the fear that they might not come across him, or that they might be too late.

"I told him to go home two hours ago," John Farrell fretted in the way that men fret who are used to having their order obeyed. "He was blue with cold even then. These blizzards are deceptive to them that don't know this country."

But when they got to Pieter Ashjian's fence and passed through the gate that Pieter had made, they found him close to the fence, stumbling along on foot with a sheep in his arms. They closed around him in a circle, reining in and holding their lanterns high.

It was Frank Sutton who spoke first. "Sheep!" he exclaimed, disgust strong in his tone. "The man carries his sheep to shelter, one by one—and on foot! I admire a thrifty man, but that's plain penny miserly! A steer is worth 10 sheep, but even a steer ain't worth riskin' a man's life for on a night like this!"

"Stop it, Frank!" John Farrell growled.

But Pieter Ashjian had heard. He dropped the sheep to the snow in front of him and stood, swaying groggily. "Pennies?" he exclaimed, his voice hoarse with anger. "Who speaks of money? Your cattle, they can shift pretty well in a storm. They drift to shelter. But sheep? When the snow comes they lie down to die where they are. And when your animals are helpless, you owe them all the help they need!"

He staggered and went to his knees, but struggled back to his feet and went on talking in slow, jerky phrases. "Money! You talk of money! Why you— You men ain't–ain't responsible! You wouldn't last a–a year back in the Old Country! We'd run you out!" He staggered again, and this time slumped forward over the limp form of the sheep and lay still.

John Farrell rose high in his stirrups and looked around the group, his eyes scornful and imperious. "You, Joe, get this man over your saddle and take him to my house. Tell the women to get him thawed out and go on with the party without us. Tell them we men will be busy and won't be back in time."

* * *

Mary Farrell did a good job on Pieter Ashjian, the task being nowise new to her. She set him down in the kitchen, wrapped in a blanket and with his feet in a washtub, and she and Hilda Ashjian rubbed his arms and legs and chapped cheeks with snow, while fat old Ed Gaines, the bunk house cook, wheezed in and out the door with fresh tubs full of snow.

The two women worked steadily, first with snow then with cold water, and as they worked shouts and laughter of the children at their games came from the front of the house. Mary Farrell made a hot toddy for Pieter Ashjian and stood over him while he drank it, and by the time Ed Gaines had to quit and go get into his Santa Claus costume, Pieter Ashjian was ready to get back into his dry clothes and boots.

She placed Pieter Ashjian in a chair at one side of the big fireplace, a precautionary blanket around his shoulders though he was again fully dressed. Hilda Ashjian sat down opposite him on the other side of the fireplace and looked at him and smiled her pleasant, slow smile. Little Piet got up from a corner where a group of smaller children were playing and came and stood at her knee. Hilda Ashjian laid a hand lightly on his shoulder and leaned down and whispered to him, and her warm smile took in all the mothers seated around the room.

Mary Farrell thought of the lonely little sod hut just around the bend of the bluff at the south end of the valley, and was glad that things had turned out as they had, though in some back corner of her mind she wondered what John would have to say about her going against his decision.

Noreen Sutton got up and started blowing out the lamps, and Florence Cullum and Lucy Whately lighted long tapers and began touching them to the candles on the tree. When they were all lighted, there was a knock at the door, and 9-year-old Joe Whately opened it.

Hilda Ashjian leaned over and spoke to Little Piet in her low, pleasant voice. "*Senen Sie, liebchen.* Look. Kriss Kringle!"

Joe Whately closed the door behind the costumed Ed Gaines and turned importantly. "That ain't Kriss Kringle," he stated positively. "That's Santa Claus."

Mary Farrell looked quickly toward Hilda Ashjian, ready to reprove the boy's rudeness. But Hilda Ashjian was smiling placidly "*Ja,*" she said. "Saint Nicholas, Sa'nt Nick-laus, Kriss Kringle—they are all the same. But now that we are Americans, we should say Santa Claus, no?"

The children gathered in a circle while Santa approached the tree and began taking down presents, reading the names and handing them out to the children. Again the room was filled with joyous noise as wrappings were stripped off and the toys displayed. But presently Mary Farrell noticed that Little Piet had withdrawn from the group and returned to his mother's knee where he stood watching as, one by one, the presents were lifted down and placed in eager hands.

With sudden awareness, Mary Farrell looked at the tree. There were only a few presents left on it. "Wait!" she exclaimed, and moved across the room. She drew Santa Claus to one side and whispered in his ear. Then she took her place again in the circling fringe of mothers as Santa returned to the tree, removed two packages, and crumpled the name tags in the palm of his hand. He turned.

"Little Piet Ashjian!" he announced, and held them out to the child.

Mary Farrell felt a warm, happy glow about her heart as Little Piet gave voice to a quick, astonished crow and stepped forward.

But suddenly Pieter Ashjian exclaimed "No!" and rose from his chair.

Mary Farrell turned, and stood squarely in his path. Her eyes met his. "Yes," she said, and laid a hand on his arm.

Pieter Ashjian's broad face was working. "You do not understand. You do not know. Tonight I have insulted your menfolks. I have called them names. You take care of me, yes. You would do that for anyone. But presents for my child, no. Your menfolks would not like that."

The room was silent. Still Mary Farrell held Pieter Ashjian's gaze. She shook her head slowly. "Pieter Ashjian," she said, "Christmas is for children. Strife and sorrow reach us all too soon. Whatever trouble there may be among you men, don't let it reach down and touch your child's happiness on this Christmas Eve."

Peter Ashjian's dark eyes were troubled. He glanced once at Little Piet, stretching out his chubby hands for the presents then back at Mary Farrell.

"Pieter." It was Hilda Ashjian's voice that broke in, and there was pleading in it. "Pieter, *Dies sind gute Leute*. These are good people."

Pieter Ashjian swallowed slowly. Then slowly he nodded. "She is right," he said huskily. "You are good people." And he turned back to his chair.

The interrupted commotion began again as Santa Claus passed out the remaining presents. Presently the jingle of sleigh bells outside announced that the bobsled had arrived and it was time for the customary midnight ride through the valley and the carol singing. The front door opened, and old Sam Webb, the Boxed-F foreman, stepped in.

"Everybody get ready," he said. "John says for everybody to see the Ashjians home, an' you can drop off at your houses on the way back."

Mary Farrell placed the Ashjians with herself on the broad seat of the bobsled, beside the driver. Behind them, seated on soft hay in the body of the sled and covered warmly with buffalo robes, rode the carolers, half a dozen of the valley women whose voices blended well and who practiced together for weeks before each Christmas Eve. Pieter Ashjian's saddle horse was tied at the end of the sled, and behind came the wagons and buckboards in which the families had come to the party.

The night was cold and clear, with frosty stars glittering in the sky; the snow creaked under the sled runners. Mary Farrell pulled the robe up tight under her chin then laid her hand in her lap. Soon Little Piet's chubby little fist snuggled into it. Mary Farrell looked ahead through the darkness and winced again at thought of the forlorn little sod hut that these people called home, and the unfinished log house that would have been so weather-tight and comfortable if Pieter Ashjian had managed to get it finished. She thought of John and wondered why he had sent the order he did, then decided that the men had probably been caring for Pieter Ashjian's sheep and would join their families there and ride home in their wagons, leading their weary saddle horses behind.

The carolers lifted their voices in the old familiar "Silent Night;" and beside her, on the other side of Little Piet, Hilda Ashjian joined in under her breath with a sweet, low-voiced alto, singing the words she knew:

"*Stille Nacht, heilige Nacht.*
Alles schloft, einsam Wacht. . . ."

And suddenly Mary Farrell realized that this woman beside her, returning to her sod hut, was happy, happy in possession of her child and her sturdy man, and in the future stretching before them. She recalled with sudden vividness her own first Christmas Eve in Silver Creek Valley, spent in the pole lean-to with her man and her

infant son, and remembered that it had been poignantly happy. . . .

The carolers sang "It Came Upon a Midnight Clear" and "Hark, the Herald Angels Sing," and interspersed the carols with old familiar hymns. The children in the wagons and buckboards took up the tunes and joined their voices with the carolers. They were singing "O Come, All Ye Faithful" when Pieter Ashjian noticed the light at the south end of the valley and exclaimed over it. Mary Farrell had been watching it for some time as they drew nearer and nearer to Pieter Ashjian's claim, and wondered about it. It came from just around the bend near the bluff, close to where Pieter Ashjian's sod hut stood. The men would need a bonfire to light them as they got the sheep and cattle to shelter, but not so big a fire as that. . . .

"What is it?" she asked, turning to Sam Webb.

But old Sam Webb merely shook the reins to make the horses go faster and said, "Wait and see." Mary Farrell detected a chuckle in his voice.

Presently they passed through the gate in Pieter Ashjian's fence, and when they rounded the bend close to the bluff, Sam Webb was plying the whip, and they covered the last few rods in fine style and drew up in a spray of lifting snow.

Mary Farrell saw, and instantly understood. Her heart leaped into her mouth, and she turned to look at Pieter Ashjian. A kind of wordless cry broke from him and he stood up, throwing the robe from around his shoulders.

"What—" he stammered hoarsely, "what is this?"

John Farrell stepped out from the group of grinning

men about the huge bonfire and stood close to the sled, smiling up at the homesteader. "Welcome, Pieter Ashjian," he said. "Welcome home."

"But–but—" Pieter Ashjian stammered. "The house. My house. You have finished it! The walls are done, and the roof is on!"

John Farrell nodded. "The snow is swept out, and there's some furniture inside, too," he replied. "Just stuff that we gathered up at some of the nearer ranch houses, things that could be spared. But they're stout and useful."

Pieter Ashjian clambered down from the wagon and stood looking up into John Farrell's smiling blue eyes. "Why?" he demanded hoarsely, his face working. "I insulted you fellows. I called you names. And then— you did this for me. Why? Why?"

John Farrell's expression was sober now. He met Pieter Ashjian's gaze squarely and swallowed before he spoke. All the wagons and buckboards were emptying now, and folks crowded around in a circle. Mary Farrell stepped in close to her husband, her eyes shining. The carolers had gathered in a group, and their voices lifted with the words, "*While shepherds watched their flocks by night.*"

John Farrell swallowed again and nodded toward the group of carolers. "That's it," he stated. "Flocks by night. You spent your precious daylight hours pushing our steers to shelter because your fence stopped 'em, then had to grope around after dark to save your sheep."

Suddenly he reached out and took Pieter Ashjian's hand. "That house would have been up by first frost, neighbor, if we'd had sense enough to know a good man when we were staring him right in the face."

Mary Farrell looked at Pieter Ashjian. Tears were streaming down his face. That was all right, for Pieter Ashjian had not yet learned the American shame at betraying deep feelings. But there was a suspicious mist in her husband's eyes, too, and his jaw was tight set.

Her own throat was tight and aching. She stepped in close, close, pressing her face against the rough collar of his coat so that he could bury his misted eyes in her hair and not stand openly shamed before all of Silver Creek Valley—his valley.

A Cake of Pink Soap

Author Unknown

Freddy Hammel and his family were, quite literally, "just off the boat," thus he didn't yet know how to act like an American. To say nothing of speaking like an American.

Now it was Christmas, and funny Freddie was giving Teacher a cake of pink soap. How rich! They teased him unmercifully every recess.

And then came the big day.

Miss Bell's lovely face glowed as she glanced down at the many Christmas gifts piled on her desk. It had become the custom in the Warrenville school for each child to bring teacher a gift the day before Christmas: a large box of monogrammed stationery from Henry Gordon; lovely handkerchiefs, some with hand-embroidered flowers and dainty lace, from Sally, Rose, Sue, and Jane; perfume from Elizabeth; a carved letter opener from Dale; and a hand-painted scarf from Theodore.

Again and again, Miss Bell reached across her desk and took one of the gifts from the pile. She would unwrap it and hold it high for the entire class to see and admire. Then she would voice her thanks and wish the donor a Merry Christmas filled with much joy and happiness.

Finally she selected one of the smallest. So intent was she on opening the box that she didn't notice the wide grins on the faces of many of the boys and girls. Some of them even snickered and moved impatiently to the edge of their seats, eager for her to see the contents. They had watched Frederick very carefully that morning, taking special notice of the size and shape of his gift. Then, they could hardly have missed it, for it was the only box wrapped in pink tissue paper and tied with a pink ribbon.

Frederick sat very still in his seat far back in the center of the room. He knew why the boys and girls were watching Miss Bell with special interest. He knew they were all waiting eagerly to burst forth with wild laughter when she held up his gift: a cake of pink soap.

Henry had been in the store that Saturday afternoon and had seen Frederick buy the soap. He had laughed when Frederick asked the clerk for a "cake of pink soap." Any boy who used pink soap, Henry told him, was less than a sissy. Without a second thought, Frederick declared in his awkward way that the soap was not for him but for Miss Bell's Christmas gift.

By the time school began on Monday morning, all the boys and girls knew that Miss Bell was going to receive a cake of pink soap as a Christmas gift from "funny Freddie." That's what the class called Frederick. He had been so nicknamed the very first day he appeared in school wearing full pantaloons and a stiff, white shirt with a large black silk scarf tied around his neck under his high, pointed collar. That was scarcely a week after Frederick and his mother and father were dismissed from Ellis Island.

It had cost Frederick's parents much more than they had planned for the three of them to come to their new home in America. Money, therefore, was very scarce in their little household for many months after their arrival in the new country.

When Frederick found out that each pupil remembered the teacher at Christmas, he was determined that he, too, would bring her a gift. For in Holland a gift meant the giver had great love for the receiver. Surely Frederick loved his teacher very much. Had not Miss Bell been very kind and patient with him, and tried in every way to help him learn how to read and write and speak English? Of course, he and his parents had studied before coming to America, but somehow English words that they had been taught in Holland were pronounced and used quite differently here in America.

Then, too, Miss Bell had spent many evenings with his mother and father, helping them become better acquainted with the language, customs, and dress of their new country.

The only thing that troubled Frederick was the fact that he didn't have much money to spend for Miss Bell's gift. In fact, he had but 10 cents. Several days after school he walked up and down Main Street, studying each shop window, but nothing could be purchased for such a small amount that would be a suitable gift for

someone he loved as much as his teacher.

Then, just last Saturday, he saw a window piled high with fairly large cakes of lovely, pink, rose-scented soap. And only 10 cents! Suddenly his dark eyes sparkled. The very thing for Miss Bell's Christmas present!

Hurrying into the store, he failed to notice it was the one owned by Henry's father. Perhaps he didn't even know it was, Henry's father's store, but such small details were of no importance to Frederick. The only thing that mattered was obtaining one of the fragrant cakes of pink soap.

All week the boys, and even some of the girls, had teased him at recess. "Funny Freddie and his pink soap!" they shouted at him. But he didn't mind. The gift was for Miss Bell—not for them. He hoped his teacher would be pleased with it.

Carefully, Miss Bell removed the lid. Then she gave a gasp of surprise and delight. She took the little white card from the box and read aloud: "To Miss Bell, my dear teacher, wishing her much joy on the Christ Child's birthday. Frederick Hammel."

There was something about the tone of Miss Bell's voice and the gleam in her brown eyes that seemed to quiet the restless group. Without being told, the boys and girls knew that something other than a plain cake of pink soap lay between the folds of the pink tissue paper. Miss Bell was lifting something from the box very slowly and very carefully. For a moment she held it in the palm of her hand and studied it with admiring eyes.

"It's lovely, Frederick," she said, smiling at him across the room. "It is truly beautiful! I have never before seen such a perfect rose carved from soap."

Then suddenly her dark eyes gleamed as she remembered two recent evenings spent with Frederick's father and mother. While the three of them bent over the grammar near the fireplace, Frederick worked quietly but diligently in the farthest corner. He was already at work when she arrived, and when she left he was so interested that on both occasions Miss Bell purposely did not go near the corner where he sat lest she disturb him.

"You carved this for me, didn't you, Frederick?" she asked in her quiet way. "My, it must have taken many long hours of patient and careful work!"

Frederick hung his head modestly. In his broken English he told her that in Holland a gift is a token of love and appreciation, especially if it is made by the giver himself.

Instead of merely holding it before the class, Miss Bell walked up and down the aisles for each child to see individually. As the boys and girls looked at the petals and leaves of the beautifully carved rose, they saw a new classmate and companion. Funny Freddy, the little Dutch boy, no longer existed. In his place was a new friend, Frederick Hammel, the little lad from Amsterdam, Holland, who had much to teach them.

A Very Special Present

Ingrid Tomey

Yes, his grandfather spoiled him—spoiled him dreadfully! And this Christmas he was going to spoil him some more.

Then they saw the crowd outside the music shop.

It's snowing today, the Saturday before Christmas. The big flakes gently touch earth, covering a lawn that is already white. There is no desperation in the falling of the snow. It is a certain promise: a white Christmas.

So it was, the Saturday before Christmas, some 30 years ago. Then I stood at the front window, a small boy watching the snow keep its Christmas promise. But it wasn't the snow—it wasn't even the delight of Christmas—that held me to the frosted glass. I was waiting for someone. And all my mother's admonitions couldn't convince me that my vigil was hopeless. I remember the moment when the big blue nose of the Hudson swung into view, and I pressed my face against the cold glass for him to see. I laughed out loud as the car sashayed around the icy corner and came to a stop on our front lawn.

The car door flung wide, and I watched the head turn toward the house. From the recesses of the bushy white beard a smile broke. He had seen me.

I couldn't help myself. I scrambled out the front door without a bathrobe, or even slippers, and galloped toward him through the six-inch snow. "Bush!" I hollered, leaping into his arms and wrapping myself around his ponderous middle. "She said you'd never come today. Mama said you wouldn't because of the snow."

"Not come!" he hollered back. "A blizzard wouldn't keep me away!" He yanked his outside black wool coat around me. "Let's get you back inside before she spots you all undressed like this." Locking me in his embrace, he bounded for the front door like a mother kangaroo.

But we weren't quick enough. Mama had spied us. "Jesse, are you crazy? Half-naked in this weather?"

I felt sheepish as she frowned at me from an upstairs window. Then she turned on Bush. "Course he's crazy. He's your grandson, isn't he? You drive all the way out here in a galloping snowstorm without snow tires, and Jesse runs through it in his bare feet. The two of you are from the same mold," she observed sharply before pushing down the window.

Oh, if only she was right! Closed in Bush's arms, his heart beating against my own, I felt almost a part of him, the most extravagant and loving human being in my 8-year-old frame of reference.

"All right!" he bellowed, tramping snow into the living room. "Who wants to go Christmas shopping?"

I released my grip around his neck and held up my

hand. "Five minutes—I'll be ready in five minutes!" I darted toward my room.

"Wait!" He threw me a package. "Merry week before Christmas!"

I carefully undid the fancy foil and set it aside for Mama to press out. The present was a shiny jackknife, the kind with umpteen blades. "Wowie-zowie! I can play mumblety-peg and carve my name under the bridge and stick apples and—"

"He already has a jackknife, Bush," Mama cut in. "In fact, he has three." She looked up from the closet where she had been trying to restore order to the garments that had fallen to the onslaught of the great black coat. "And he has three kites, four yo-yos, and heaven knows how many bags of marbles."

Bush waved me off to get dressed while she ticked off the list of his indulgences. She was moved to state these simple truths every Saturday when he arrived with my gift. She had long since given up pleading with him to stop bringing them. Perhaps her words were really for my instruction. As if by growing up in a fatherless household I didn't already know the difference between a necessity and an extravagance.

I pulled my sweater over my head and waited to hear him tell her, "Jesse is my whole life, Nette. You think a few jackknives are going to ruin him? Well, if so, *I'll* ruin him. But he's going to know I love him more than anything on God's earth."

Oh, how wonderful that made me feel—to be loved the best in all the world! I leaned against my bedroom door and hugged myself in pure joy.

We did go shopping that day, taking Mama's list as we passed through the door. "If you must buy him something, Bush, refer to this list. These are the things he needs."

Bush snatched the list and stuffed it in his cavernous pocket, never to be consulted again.

Then Mama pulled me back through the door by the belt of my coat. "No stuffed snakes, or bears, or tigers," she cautioned, pointing at the black departing shape.

"OK, Mama."

And we escaped.

* * *

In town the streets were crowded with shoppers. Bush and I disembarked and stood briefly, surveying the hordes bumping along with their bright packages. Clutching his beard in his great paw, he frowned at me. "Jesse, you'd be in peril on the sidewalk today. One of these fancy ladies is likely to snatch you away to be a Christmas doll for her little girl." And with one grand sweep of his arms, he lifted me onto his shoulders.

So, Rajah-like, I rode six feet above the crowds, who waved and saluted when they saw me riding the incarnation of Santa Claus down Main Street. Overhead, red plastic bells swung from silver tinsel at every lamppost. Snowflakes brushed my cheeks. Christmas was in the air, and I was eager to seek it out. "To the dime store," I commanded, and my sumpter bounced off in the direction of toyland, pausing only long enough to exchange waves with me in the reflection of every plate-glass window that we passed.

Bush bought us some cinnamon red hots at the dime-store candy counter, and my mouth and tongue burned with their spicy sharpness as we explored the aisles. He paused by the stuffed animals.

"That's a dandy tyrannosaurus," he observed, testing me.

I studied the giant, two-footed monster of green and yellow and shook my head. "Mama would never let us back in the house with it."

So we moved over to the stacks of Chinese checkers and Monopoly® games. Bush picked up a game of Flinch®. "You want this?"

"You already bought me that game last summer."

"Mmmmmmmm," he uttered, tugging on his beard as though stymied. He briefly fingered an artful pyramid of encyclopedias but pronounced them "joyless."

We seemed to be at an impasse. "Bush, what can we do—we've looked at everything." I stared disconsolately at my bright red, sticky fingers. I had finished the red hots. We had completed the dime-store circuit.

He tipped back his shaggy head and sniffed the air as though on a scent. "Ahhh." He pulled his beard fiercely in apparent thought. "Hum, hum, hum." Then, tentatively, "You probably wouldn't want to but— No, never mind." He waved the thought away.

I assailed the hoary head with my sticky hands. "What, Bush, what?"

"Peabody's?" he asked in an exaggerated whisper.

The bike shop. So he had been teasing me all along. With a squeal I hugged the woolly beard as we rushed back out into the stream of shoppers. And that would have been the end of it, for, of course, the red-and-chrome two-wheeler in Peabody's window was what I really wanted. But we had to pass the music shop to get to Peabody's. And passing that shop changed everything, not only for Christmas but, in a way, forever.

"Why are all those people standing outside the music shop?" I asked as we approached.

"Ah. They're lining up to get a gander at the most beautiful boy north of Antarctica," he said, lovingly squeezing the toes of my galoshes.

"No, look! There's a little girl in there, playing the piano." I could see her seated in front of a shiny little spinet. She was wearing a red dress and had a red bow in her hair. It seemed to me that her hands danced over the keys like two butterflies. She played like the great Liberace. I reached down and lifted Bush's earflap. "Listen, you can hear her." Soft strains of "O Holy Night" filtered through to the street.

Bush inclined his head. "She plays like Nette," he murmured.

"Mama?" I had never heard her play.

Suddenly Bush rapped his knuckles against the windows until the little girl looked up. "'Greensleeves!'" he thundered through the pane.

She nodded, and dutifully thumbed through her sheet music. Presently the old carol floated through to the street.

Bush spoke to my reflection in the glass. "Your mama played that every Christmas morning. We could hear her downstairs, soft as a dream. And then, if we didn't leap out of bed, she would play louder and louder." I could feel his shoulders start to shake with laughter. "Hah!" he gasped. "She rousted us out of bed while the stars were still out, and she made us stand in the parlor and sing Christmas carols before we could have so much as a glimpse of the breakfast table."

I tried to picture Mama as a young girl on Christmas morning. Did she wear a red bow in her hair? For all the mornings I could remember, she had appeared at the breakfast table dressed in brown cotton, her work uniform for Walton's Office Supply. I never saw her wear a hair bow.

"I didn't know Mama could play the piano," I said to Bush. But I was thinking about all the mornings at the breakfast table. While I wolfed down my oatmeal, Mama would listen to the radio. She would close her eyes and run her hands over the scratched blond table while Sarah Vaughan or Les Baxter crooned. I had supposed it was the same kind of pretending a boy does riding a broomstick. He never expects to own a live horse.

But I asked the question. "How much is a piano?"

He shook his head at my reflection. "Enough with pianos, Jesse. We gotta get over to Peabody's."

I glanced back at the red dress, the black piano. And my heart suddenly swelled with desire. "Couldn't we buy it for her?" I scrambled down off his shoulders and confronted him. "Think, Bush, how she'd love it."

"Love it?" he snorted. "She'd skin us alive, that's what she'd do, buying something that expensive. Besides, what she needs is an automatic washing machine, one of those gizmos without the wringers that snarl and snap apart."

"No, she'd love it," I insisted, inching toward the door.

So we went inside, "just to ask the price."

"Five hundred dollars!" Bush thumped his hands dangerously against the glass counter and turned to me in a fury. "There! You see? Only John D. Rockefeller has that kind of money."

The salesman's voice chimed brightly in the air. "You can pay $200 down, the rest in easy installments."

By that time I was desperate for the piano, and I knew with Bush all things were possible. Stuffed bears, yo-yos, coloring books, and other gifts spilled out of him as from a cornucopia. I suspected always that great wads of eager money lay within the recesses of the black coat.

Yet he was still shaking his head as he bent to confer with me. "You see, Jess, if we pay $200 then there's nothing left over. No washing machine for her, and nothing—nothing for you." His ragged brows tortured his forehead. "No bike, Jesse."

I sucked in my breath and looked into his pleading eyes. He wanted the bike for me as badly as I did. How could I possibly turn it down? For a bike I would sacrifice a year of Saturday presents.

But my eight years of cupidity rose to accuse me. Bush's steady generosity over the years had more than kept pace with my desires. I had as much booty as other 8-year-olds of more comfortable means. Mama, on the other hand, received only the most utilitarian of gifts: bedroom slippers, calendars, washing machines—nothing foolish with red bows on it, nothing to make her

squeal with delight.

"I want the piano," I whispered into his beard.

So he paid the $200 and signed some papers about the balance while I chose as many sheets of Christmas carols as my 75 cents would buy. "Be sure to deliver these in the bench," I instructed, alerting the salesman that I was wise to the other uses of piano benches.

Then we walked back out into the cheerful traffic, with empty pockets and only one Christmas gift. My heart was singing, full of love for Bush and myself and the wonder of our splendid gift. And I kept trying to picture Mama's happy face on Christmas morning. I slapped my hands in rhythm against the cold blue car seat. "Here comes Santa Claus; here comes Santa Claus!" I chortled.

As we pulled onto our street, Bush looked at me out of puzzled eyes. "What will I give you for Christmas?"

* * *

During the days before Christmas, Bush and I bought and trimmed the tree and hung mistletoe in doorways. The piano arrived on schedule while Mama was at work, and we had the delivery men put it in the extra bedroom where Bush was sleeping. I cautioned Mama not to enter for fear of discovering one of my Christmas projects which I professed to be working on. I even scattered bits of colored paper outside in the hallway to lend authenticity to the fib.

Bush grumbled that the piano hogged the bedroom and bumped into him at night.

After what seemed like weeks of waiting, Christmas dawned with the clacking of frozen holly against my window. I threw off my covers and rushed down the hall to coax Mama and Bush awake. "Today's the day!" I whispered to Bush conspiratorially.

The three of us gathered under the glowing tree and exchanged our gifts. Mama had made me another bathrobe and presented it with a matching pair of felt slippers. There were candies and nuts from a Florida uncle, and a game of jacks from some distant cousins.

Finally Bush and I exchanged our gifts. I had covered a soup can with green foil: a pencil holder, according to my teacher. "A cigar holder!" Bush proclaimed, ceremoniously stuffing it full of fat cigars. Then he held out a present the size of a shoe box. "I love you, Jesse"—he drew me close and whispered in my ear—"as much as a red Schwinn bike."

The present was another stuffed animal, a small black leopard with yellow glass eyes. "This is nifty, Bush. And I don't even have a leopard," I reminded him.

His expression was pained, so I said no more. I climbed up on his lap and watched while Mama opened my homemade calendar and a big fruitcake from the Florida relatives, and finally some gloves from Mr. Walton at the office supply store.

After she had admired everything, Mama smoothed out her blue robe. "Hasn't this been a nice Christmas, though?"

I nodded and hugged myself tightly to keep from exploding.

Then she smiled at me. "And you and your grandfather are starving for breakfast, right?"

I shook my head and stood up. The moment had finally come, and I was tongue-tied. "M-mama," I stammered. "There's something–" I gulped, looking at Bush for help.

"Just show her, Jesse," he growled, motioning me to the bedroom with his cigar.

So I slipped my hand in hers and led her down the hall to Bush's room. My hands shook as I turned the knob and pushed open the door.

I didn't look at the piano. I looked at Mama. The faint, expectant smile left her face and she stood frozen in the doorway, squeezing my hands as if in fear. She opened her mouth but nothing came out. She just stared at the little black spinet crowded next to the bed.

Where were the shrieks of joy? "Mama," I pointed out, "it's a piano."

Then she looked at me, and I could see she wasn't afraid, only amazed. "Is it for *me?*" she whispered.

I nodded vigorously, too swollen with love and pride to answer.

She took a deep breath and tried to smile at me, but two tears came trickling down her cheeks.

"Don't cry, Mama!" I buried myself in the blue robe. "It's for you—it really is." But I knew why she was crying. She knew the piano was for her. She knew we had bought her a foolishly extravagant Christmas present that cost more than an automatic washer and dryer put together and was something she didn't need but the only thing she had ever wanted.

Oh, what delirious joy there was for me standing there with Mama's arms around me, happier than I had ever seen her. That I could bring her such joy was revelation. Tears sprang to my own eyes. "Do you love it, Mama?" I asked, looking at her.

She nodded. "I love you, Jesse." Then she turned to Bush, who was smoking furiously behind us. "And I love you, Pa." She reached over and kissed his woolly cheek.

Glowering, he pointed his cigar at the piano. "We paid to hear music. Let's see if you still remember how to play this thing."

I rushed to the bench importantly. "The music is in here." I lifted the lid and fanned out my assortment of Christmas music. "I chose these myself," I said, preening in my glory.

I can still hear those first songs that she played so gingerly, as if afraid of desecrating the piano with a wrong note.

"Faster, Mama," I urged. "We want to sing."

And we sang "It Came Upon a Midnight Clear," Bush and I in the doorway with our arms about each other, while I envisioned angels bending to accompany us on golden harps.

Then I said, "Remember how you used to play 'Greensleeves' on Christmas morning?" And Mama laughed like a young girl and sorted through the music until she found it.

So we stopped singing to listen, and I leaned against Bush and let the Christmas feeling soak into my bones. I looked up at him, and he smiled half-heartedly back at me.

He was happy for Mama, I knew he was. But he was like Balthazar without a gift, bereft of his purpose. How could I tell him that the bike he didn't give me for Christmas that year was a greater gift than all the bikes and marbles of my childhood?

* * *

As I watched this December snowfall, our little Christmas so many years ago keeps unfolding its secrets to me, a timeless epiphany of love. And of sorrow too, for it signaled the departure of childhood and simple truths. But I have not outgrown my belief in Santa Claus, that jolly spirit of giving. I can almost see him beyond my window, striding through a million snowflakes in his great black coat, counting the days until Christmas.

Bless the Child

Isobel Stewart

Simon was dead, but was that any reason for her to be so cold to her own husband, to her own daughter? And then this new baby. No! She absolutely refused to make a polite call on the family!

Until one particular night.

Most of the time it was all right, as long as she was busy. If she could fill every moment from morning till night, and then be so tired she would collapse, there was no time to think.

Or to remember.

And that was a strange thing, Sarah would find herself thinking. Sometimes the last thing she wanted was to remember, but there were times when she longed to recapture those sunny golden days before her baby had died. The warm, heavy feeling of a sleeping baby in her arms, the joy of watching him wake, of waiting for his smile. He had been only a year old, such a small child, she sometimes thought, to have left such a huge emptiness in her life.

In all their lives, she would remind herself. There was a shadow in John's eyes that had never been there before, and Rebecca was too quiet, too serious for a lit-

tle girl of 6. The grandparents, too, missed Simon and grieved for him.

They hadn't spoken about Simon, she and John, since the day he died. John had tried, many times, but she couldn't find words for her grief and her loss. Now, in the last few weeks, he had stopped trying, and she was grateful for that. Sometimes she would look at her husband, and at their small daughter, and she would remind herself that she was very lucky to have John and Rebecca, and they were still a family, after all.

But now that almost a year had passed and John went about his work and Rebecca played with friends, Sarah thought sometimes that she was the only one who still mourned for her baby. It did help, keeping busy, and she didn't mind that their inn was not only fully booked but overflowing, and there was cooking and cleaning and organizing to be done every minute of every day.

"Are you all right, Sarah?" John asked, coming in to find her baking bread, her face flushed from the oven heat. "You look tired."

"I'm fine," she assured him, and she really meant it.

But there was still concern on his face. "Only a few days longer, this busy time," he said, and for a moment his hand covered hers. "Then I'll see that you have a rest."

With an effort, she smiled. "I'm fine," she told him again. "You'd better get back to your thirsty customers. Where's Rebecca?"

He hesitated but only for a moment. "I think she's with the baby," he said, evenly.

Sarah tried to keep her voice even too. "She really

does spend too much time with those people, and we know nothing about them, John. Tell her I need her to help me."

He nodded, and went out without saying anything, although Sarah knew he had wanted to protest.

Five minutes later Rebecca came in, slowly, reluctantly. "I was helping to look after the baby," she said softly.

Sarah went on kneading the dough. "I'm sure his mother can do that," she told the child. "Just clean these dishes for me, Rebecca."

Obediently, small as she was, Rebecca began to wash the dishes. "Mommy," she said after a moment, "I want to give the baby a present, a special present, because he's a special baby."

For a moment, Sarah's hands were still. "All babies

73

are special," she said, and she tried to keep the bitterness from her voice.

"But this one is very special," Rebecca murmured. "You should come and see him, Mommy. He's so sweet, and his mother is so nice. When I told her about Simon, she said—"

Sarah whirled around. "When you told her *what?*" she asked, her voice unsteady.

The color left Rebecca's small face. "I told her about Simon," she said. Her eyes were anxious but she didn't look away. "I told her how he used to laugh when I played with him, and I told her he had only four teeth, and he was just learning to walk, and—"

After a pause Rebecca went on, very softly. "It was nice, talking about Simon. Both the grannies cry when I want to talk about him, but the baby's mother liked hearing about him. Are you angry, Mommy?"

"No, Rebecca, I'm not angry," Sarah said. But the small face looking up into hers was still anxious, and she bent down and hugged her daughter. Rebecca's arms held on to her tightly, and Sarah knew, with sadness, that this was something she did all too seldom now. "Run along," she told the little girl.

At the door, Rebecca turned. "Do you want to see the baby?" she asked.

"No," Sarah said quickly, "I'm much too busy to come." *No,* she thought, when Rebecca had gone, her feet dancing across the dusty sunlit courtyard, *I'm not prepared to do that, to see this young woman with her baby, holding him the way I held Simon, feeding him, dreaming dreams for him, the way I did. And not knowing, either, what the future holds for her child.*

"Quite obsessed with those people, she is," she told her husband that night, when Rebecca was asleep. "She talks about them all the time. She says she wants to give the baby a present."

He looked at her across the kitchen table. "It would mean a lot to her, love, if you would just go with her and say hello to them. They're a nice little family. And they may be going away very soon." His voice was cautious now. "It may be wiser for them. You know the people who came to see them? They said—"

"Look, John, I don't want to know anything about them," Sarah said, all the vague doubts and worries crystallizing. "There's too much going on that's very strange, and I don't want us getting mixed up in anything political. We were only doing them a kindness, taking them in. If you ask me, the sooner they go the better."

The better for all of us, she told herself determinedly the next day, ignoring the smudge of tears on Rebecca's face when she was refused permission to go and see the baby and his mother.

"But I won't see them again if they go away," Rebecca said, and Sarah looked at her small daughter, taken aback by a new determination in her face and in her voice.

"Who said anything about them going?" she asked, instinctively lowering her voice.

"I heard Daddy telling you last night," Rebecca said. "If they do go, Mommy, please let me give the baby a special present."

"And what do you want to give this baby?" Sarah asked, only half her attention now on the child.

"I want to give him Simon's teething ring,"

Rebecca said clearly. "The one that Grandpa made for him out of bone and shiny stuff."

"Silver, the shiny stuff," Sarah replied, managing to keep her voice steady. "You want to give him Simon's teething ring?" *The only thing I have left*, she thought, *with the marks of his little teeth on it.* The long-suppressed tears were suddenly very close.

"We don't need it now," Rebecca said. "This baby hasn't any teeth yet, but when he does, he could put it on his sore gums the way Simon did, and it would help, and–and I think our Simon would like the baby to have it."

She's only a child, Sarah reminded herself; *she doesn't know what it is she's asking.* "No, Rebecca," she said firmly "You can't give Simon's teething ring to this baby. I don't want to hear another word about it."

Through the rest of that day Rebecca didn't mention either the baby or the special gift she wanted to give him. But often Sarah would find the child's eyes resting on her. *Almost*, Sarah thought a little uncomfortably, *as if she's waiting for something.*

That night John woke her soon after midnight.

"What is it?" she asked, sleepy, bewildered. "Is something wrong?"

"They're going," he said simply, and she knew whom he meant. "They have to go right away, before morning, Sarah. Please come and see them, before they go."

In the dim light she looked up at him. *He asks so little of me*, she thought, painfully. *He is a good man, an uncomplaining, patient man, and Simon was his son too.* For the first time, in all the months of their loss, she admitted to herself how she had shut him out, held her loss close to her, and never really tried to understand that it was his loss too.

"All right, I'll come," she murmured, pulling a robe around her. As she spoke, he was waking Rebecca, murmuring something to her.

In the still of the night they went across the courtyard quietly, and Sarah, suddenly shy and uncomfortable, let her husband and her daughter go in ahead of her. There was very little light in the stable, but she could see the manger where the baby had slept. He was in his mother's arms now, as she sat on the straw. The father stood behind them, big, quiet, protective.

John and Rebecca were waiting for her, and they went across the stable together, toward the little family. And then, before they reached the baby, they stopped, all three of them. Sarah, uncomprehending, knew only that she *had* to stop. She never knew how long they stood there, with the stillness and the wonder around them, before they knelt down.

"I didn't know," Sarah murmured, awed. "I didn't know who He was. I didn't understand before."

There was so little time. Time for the young mother, Mary, to let her kiss the baby's tiny hand, time for her to let Sarah know, in a strange, wordless way, that she understood about Simon but that Sarah mustn't shut her heart to the rest of her family. There was a moment for Sarah to tell Rebecca to run across and bring Simon's teething ring for the baby, a moment for John to give the father, Joseph, some provisions for the journey.

"Be on your way as quickly as you can," John said,

"For His safety."

They watched as the little family left the inn in the moonlight, the mother and the child on the donkey, the father walking beside them.

And when they were out of sight, Sarah and her husband and her child turned to go back to their own room. *Everything has changed*, Sarah thought with awe. *I have changed. John has changed. Perhaps the whole world has changed.*

"Look," Rebecca said, softly.

They followed her gaze upward, to the star, clear and bright in the sky above the stable.

"It's been there all the time," she told them. "Ever since He was born."

Star-spangled Christmas

Kathleen Norris

World War II was raging across Europe, and refugees everywhere were seeking safe havens, lodging, and food. Already thousands of orphan children had overwhelmed the already under-funded orphanages.

In America a wealthy man and woman who only last Christmas had celebrated Christmas with great joy now, bereft of their two children, had no desire to celebrate Christmas. And they'd all but lost each other as well.

Then came the dread shout: "Fire! Fire at the Mills!"

How about our going away for Christmas?" Hilary suggested. She said it lightly, casually. But she didn't look at Jim. She looked down at the strip of bacon on her plate and cut it in two with her fork.

Jim was standing in the bow window of the bright, warm little breakfast room, looking out at the bare branches of trees and the glistening mounds of sugar that were the garden shrubs. He didn't turn his head as he answered her question with another. "Away from Bridgeover? Us?" he asked. "Where to?"

"Oh . . ." His wife's voice hung in the air for a second. "To New York. To—dinner somewhere. And the theater," she said.

"I see." But it was obvious that Jim didn't see. It was obvious that he was shocked and bewildered. After all, there had been Bridges at Bridgeover for more than a hundred Christmases. To think of the big house, silent and empty at Christmas time, was disturbing to him, almost frightening.

There was a brief silence in the breakfast room. Hilary, pretending to go on with her breakfast, was outwardly self-controlled, silent New England to the bone. But there had been an Irish-Scotch great-grandmother in Hilary's line, and the agony that filled her heart now was her legacy from the most emotional of all the races. To go away from home for Christmas, instead of having the roomy old house full of cousins and uncles and aunts for the great day, was to feel death touch her freshly. But they couldn't stay here! They couldn't do that. Small, fair, lovely in her stiff brocade breakfast gown, she steeled herself to continue the conversation composedly.

"I was thinking it might be—easier, Jim."

Jim cleared his throat. "Yep. Might be," he agreed. "We—we might try to sort of—to skip Christmas," he said.

Silence again in the breakfast room and in the gardens and woods where loads of snow slipped occasionally from the low boughs of the trees.

But Bridgeover, half a mile away, was not going to skip Christmas, whatever the owner of the Mills did. Christmas was some days away, yet already there could be heard shouts and cries from the children in the vil-

lage, premature horns and cowbells. No, Bridgeover would celebrate. The grief that enveloped the big house on the hill would not affect the factory workers. They would all have their fattened Christmas pay envelopes, their turkeys from the farms, their trees from the timber stretches that had supplied Christmas trees to the town for those hundred Christmases since the days of its founder. They had supplied a Christmas tree last year for Daphne and Peter.

This year Daphne and Peter had two little holly trees instead. Other women who had lost children had seen Hilary in the graveyard yesterday, white-faced and silent in furs, watching somberly while the men leveled the snow and cleared the deep-cut stone and set the little pots of polished leaves and shining berries in place.

Peter Bridges, 5 years old; Daphne Wellington Bridges, 3. Last year they had raced into their parents' room early on Christmas morning to snuggle down under warm covers in warm arms and announce that it was Christmas Day at last.

This year their covering was the pure, chill whiteness of the snow.

And the deep coldness of snow was in Jim's voice when he said, "Suppose we skip Christmas?"

Hilary had had seven months of it; added to her own pain had been the agony of his. Suffering, withdrawn, inarticulate, polite. He could not let go; he could not ease the tightness, the loneliness of his soul. He was sorry for her—oh, she knew that! He wanted in a weary, remote sort of way to help her. She knew that too. Jim was not willingly making it hard for her. But Jim was proud. And fate had struck cruelly at his pride.

There was no Bridges in the new generation. Jim's sisters, four of them, had their quivers full. Three little Frothinghams, three little Archers, four little Elliots, and two small Fishers called Jim "uncle." But Peter had been the only Bridges, and Peter's fair little tousled head had been lying very still under the soft, warm earth for many months now.

It was a fact. He and Hilary had had to take it. They had lost their children. . . . It had been natural enough for a small boy and girl to seat themselves on a grassy bank on a sunshiny May morning, their nurse knitting quietly a few yards away, to watch the trucks thundering along the lane below with loads of lumber for the new factory at the Mill, their small bare knees clasped by their small brown hands, their burnished waves of tawny hair close together in consultation. Who could have dreamed that moment to be life's last moment for the favored children of the house of Bridges? Who could have dreamed that the bank, softened by April's long rains, would slip under that light weight, would carry them on an accelerating rush of roots and grass and earth straight across the track of an oncoming leviathan of a truck?

Hilary had been a lost woman for weeks after the tragedy, hardly conscious of the plans of her four brothers, her sisters-in-law, the aunts and grandmothers, to keep her company, to help her back to sanity. The summer days, and those that followed, were one long, dark dream of being submerged, of coming to the top of the strangling waters to look wearily about at a world robbed of all interest, of sinking down into the choking black depths again. For hours she had schooled herself to greet Jim, returning hot and tired from the Mills, with a cheerful word. But the word had always drowned itself in tears. And now it was Christmas, and Hilary told herself that everything would be easier once Christmas was over.

She didn't want to go away from home for Christmas any more than Jim did. Home, with its books and pictures and familiar turns of stairway and recessed windows, was the place of all places one wanted to be. But not this year! Not this year.

"We—we needn't let anyone know where we're going," she pursued her plan. "We could go to, oh, anywhere."

"Christmas Eve," the motionless figure at the window suggested. "About noon, Christmas Eve. I'll drive the small car. Not Cass. Nobody with us."

"Christmas Eve!" she echoed.

He came over to her suddenly. Oh, he mustn't do that! He mustn't do that! The deep waters were catching her, engulfing her.

But he didn't drop to his knees and put his arms about her and let her rest her face blessedly against the roughness of his collar. The days when she might have done that, when she had had no real troubles, no real aching hunger for the shelter of his big arms, were gone. Now that she needed comfort, it was denied. She must hold back her tears and manage a smile as he said awkwardly, back in his own seat now and with his fingers over her own, "I'm so horribly sorry for you, Hilary."

The wall was still there. She could not climb it nor see through it. It shut him in with his own pain; it shut her out.

Nothing more was said. Presently Jim shook himself into his big coat and went away to the Mills.

* * *

At lunch nothing further was said of their going away. Hilary and Jim talked of the party that was planned for Christmas Eve in the schoolhouse down in the village; they speculated as to how long the snow would fall, and Jim said that a storm was gathering again.

At 2:00 he went back to the office. The snow fell. In the big empty house Hilary could sometimes hear a door open then close softly. But otherwise a dreamy silence held the place like an uncanny spell.

"We're not going to be here for Christmas Day; we're going away Christmas Eve," Hilary told her maid.

"To Mrs. Elliot's?" Abby surmised, her middle-aged face anxious and sympathetic.

"I think not. We're probably going to New York."

A silence. Then Abby turned her broad, faithful back to Hilary as she folded the wide bedspread and spoke mildly. "Better, maybe. And maybe next year," she ventured, "we'll have special company. The Lord'll send you a comforter."

No. Never that, Hilary said in her heart. Aloud she said nothing. She had said nothing during those first awful weeks when her aunts and Jim's sisters and her brothers' wives had all hinted the same thing. Terrible, terrible tragedy, darling. But then you're only 30, Hilary, and someday (not now, of course!) you'll want another baby.

And from the first moment of incredible horror, her whole being had said *no*, even though her voice never had said it.

No, she would not sell her heart to a child again. She would not go through those long months of waiting again, fill the drawers of the old walnut highboy with tiny, fluffy garments, endure the heavy last weeks lying on the couch upstairs with the bearskin drawn over her feet, through the snowy days of another Christmas. She had shrunk back in inexpressible pain from the thought of it. To Jim's hoarse "Never again!" she had added her own sob-racked whisper, "Oh, no; no, not again!"

So she said nothing to Abby, and the day wore itself to an early blue twilight over the snow. She was sitting in the library beside the fire on the afternoon of Christmas Eve, writing telegrams to all the sisters and cousins and aunts with holly-wreathed greetings, when Jim came home. Her heart gave that great spring of joy that only women's hearts know when the man comes home, but she merely looked up at him with a quiet smile as he came in and commented upon the fact that he had changed his clothes. "You must have been soaked to the skin in this sleety wind," she said.

"I was." He had sunk into his own chair. He looked at the fire, stretching chilled hands toward it. "Got the bags packed?" he asked.

"All packed. Waiting for you."

"I'm later than I thought I'd be. I was wondering— we could take the night train, of course."

"Easily." She was silent a moment. "It would be hard driving," she said. "Of course we could take the train. Or we could stay here."

She felt rather than saw the quick lift of his head; the keenness of his glance.

"Would you?" he asked in a low tone.

"If we could be alone," she answered, her voice thickening.

"They all think we are going, Hilary. No one would come. No one would telephone. We've told them all we had plans."

"Then I think I would like to stay here, Jim. I belong here. We both do."

Quiet words, quietly said. But in all the bitter months, somehow, they two had not been able to speak to each other so naturally. They had talked strangely, fighting sorrow, comforting each other's sorrow, trying to find ways not to face it, not to feel its burden upon them, not to admit that it was there. Now, man and wife, here by their saddened hearth, it was as if Sorrow herself had suddenly joined them and joined their hands, bidding them be of her sobered company, reminding them that they who mourn shall be comforted in good time.

"It is good to need each other, Jim. To have nobody else," Hilary said after a silence.

"I was thinking that," Jim said simply. He kept his eyes on the fire, but when she came to the hassock at his knee, she felt his arm laid lightly about her shoulder as it never had been laid before.

For a long time they sat so, lonely and alone in the great house on Christmas Eve, yet feeling something of a new peace in their hearts.

* * *

It was Abby who broke into their quiet time. Not the usual noiselessly-moving Abby with the evening papers to light the lamps and, perhaps, bring a message of Christmas greeting. No, this was a totally unfamiliar Abby, pale and breathless, and followed by several other members of the household staff. Hilary could only leap to her feet with a sure prescience of calamity when the dread word was among them all.

"Fire! Fire at the Mills! In among the houses, sir. We heard the shouting, and Bertha and me run out— and then the telephone rang—"

"You stay here; I'll be back!" Jim said.

"Oh, no; let me go!"

They were running toward the coat closet in the hall as they spoke, the servants in a jumble about them.

"Oh, Jim, in this wind!" Hilary said, as the car rocketed over the snowy surfaces in the blue dusk toward the billowing smoke that was already pouring from the village roofs.

If she had had any intention of waiting at the house for news it was forgotten now. She was bundled into one of Jim's coats. She was beside him as he parked the car in a straggling line of dilapidated, snow-blotched cars outside the ring of the fire, and joined the churning crowd that had gathered there. One fire engine was operating vigorously. A great arc of water shot up into the twilight and fell seething into the blowing waves of smoke. A knot of firemen were having trouble with the larger engine; it was as yet of no use.

"It's the last wooden block!" Jim said. "Oh, if we'd only taken it down in time!"

Women all about Hilary were crying and exclaiming. The fire, it appeared, had started just after the Christmas party had gotten happily under way a short half-hour ago. That it had not turned in upon the revelers was a miracle over which these women would exclaim for the rest of their lives. A hundred children in tinsel fancy dress, the loaded tree, the crowd of admiring parents, Santa Claus himself in his bush of whiskers, might all have been swept by flames, caught in a pen of terror and death.

Instead, the savage flames had turned themselves up the hill and, fanned by one of the wildest gales of the winter, had spread through a score of old wooden buildings. The last frame structures of the Mill settlement were of century-old timbers, and they were going up like so much matchwood. Along this unbroken row of dark windows, now reflecting the angry red of the blaze, and these worn doorsteps upon which four generations of foreign-born women had lingered and chatted for more than a hundred years, lived many women who had taken older children to the Christmas tree party, leaving smaller children tucked in asleep at home. These desperate mothers were threading the already excited throng, screaming, struggling to get through the lines, pleading with the firemen.

"They're all out—we've been through every room!" the men shouted back.

Crying, sympathetic neighbors took up the reassurance: "The children are all out, Mrs. O'Brien! That was Tim Carney—he just said so! He's got three of his own and a grandchild, dear; he wouldn't lie to you!"

But the comforters were almost as hysterical as the uncomforted, and in the scene that the darkening night and the strengthening gale made bedlam, Hilary rushed to and fro, now catching the arm of some distracted mother and half dragging, half pushing her toward the group of older women who were making frenzied efforts to gather the separated and crying children together; now feeling her hand grasped by some cold little strange hand, and stooping in the fearful darkness and fearful light to listen to the frightened whisper, "Please find my mother!"

For a time it was a tiny Ingeborg Svensen who clung to her. Then a big girl of 14 came up, capably, and remarked sociably, "Not much of a Christmas for us, Mrs. Bridges!" she declared then turned to Ingeborg. "Come on, Inga," she said in a soothing voice, "your aunt Selma and your mother are over here!"

The noise of the fire itself was deafening. The uproar of voices made any hope of mere talking vain. Hilary shouted and screamed with the rest. Whenever an especially high wave of flame, fringed with fountains of sparks, swept up against the sky, a roar arose from the crowd. When a roof caved in with a great up-rushing of pale blue and scarlet tongues, there was a general groan. The line of watchers wavered and changed, and sickening rumors flew on wings as swift as the swift gale.

"Captain Ranovitch went into Moretti's place and hasn't come out yet!" "They can't find the McKeogh baby!" "Mrs. Patroni's in the hospital, and they're afraid to tell her that Gemma got burned up!" "Oh, the mortality is frightful—the mortality is frightful!"

"Jim," Hilary said, stopping him as he went to and fro among the garish lights and inky shadows, "these women are saying that a lot of children have been lost—"

"No, no, no! We don't think so!" he said, unworried but abstracted. "Lenz told me they fine-combed those houses up at the end of the row before the fire got up that way. There weren't any children in the nearest places—not in the Hagopian house, nor the Fresnoys—they told me so themselves. These fellows are doing magnificent work. It won't spread now, but the old row is gone. Good thing, too! You go on getting the children together in the schoolhouse. George Moore's here somewhere—he'll take 'em in there as fast as we get 'em assorted—"

"Mr. Bridges says that no children were caught at all!" Hilary said loudly, again and again, guiding two small boys toward the improvised nursery. This was the schoolhouse now, and it hummed with heartening activity. Soot-streaked faces showed above spattered and dirty party finery; children had stopped crying, and with tear-streaked cheeks and sopping slippers were regarding the scene from playroom benches.

By this time many mothers had been appeased by the actual presence of all their children in their arms, and three or four capable women had started coffee pots to boiling in the school kitchen and were passing out slices of bread and jam, directing small boys to carry the cups out to the men and be careful, too, and otherwise seizing upon the crisis with palpable if disguised enjoyment.

They were still exchanging calamitous observations with much clucking of tongues, but the supreme terror had evaporated from the occasion, and such mothers as were to lodge for the night in the schoolhouse had seen to it that Sid Levey, the janitor, had been unearthed and got the furnaces started full blast. The room in which the deserted Christmas tree still stood brightly lighted had attracted some of the wide-eyed younger fry, who strayed in there to touch the ornaments and tinsel with wet little filthy fingers. Hilary observed that

an officious group of young girls, not more than 14 or 15, had taken matters in hand, seeing to it that the undisturbed toy pile should not be rifled, and were addressing the smaller children briskly by name:

"Olga, you go tell your mama you're with us; she was looking for you!" "Here's a busted tarlatan stocking; you kids can divide that candy." " Jean, pile these chairs along there and make a fence around the toys." "Here's somebody's purse—Mrs. McClintock! Mrs. McClintock, if anybody asks for a purse say that Helen Connor has it!" "I won't have anything to eat, thanks, Mrs. Du Quesne, until we've got those firemen fed!"

Cakes, large and small, evidently salvaged from the party, were now going the rounds. Young mothers, comfortably seated in scattered chairs, were nursing their babies and watching the animated scene with placid, bovine eyes. Every few minutes there was a stricken lull when someone came through asking if the little Harris boy and 5-year-old Gemma Patroni had been found yet, but afterward the activities in the school instantly returned to normal levels again. Blankets and cots were appearing in rapidly-established rows against a long wall. Some of the smaller children were immediately placed into them and were off to sleep at an hour that seemed midnight, but that was really nearer 8:00 than 9:00.

"Mrs. Bridges had Southerland open the store and she sent over all the blankets, and he's sending sugar and bread and everything!" said the gossips. And then at the opened door the anxious face appeared again. "Anyone seen Gemma Patroni? Little Junior Harris in here?"

At 10:00 Jim hurried in. "Hillary, Cass is here with the station wagon, and I think you'd better take the small car and go back to the house. The insurance man just arrived and wants to go about with me, and—there are still a couple of kids missing. I *think* they're all right, but I'll have to stick around until they turn up."

She caught at him with a quick grasp. "Jim, the poor mothers!"

"Yes, I know," he answered unemotionally. Jim had never been especially demonstrative, and for seven long months he had schooled himself to show no emotion at all. He showed none now.

"They're making coffee, Jim. You'll— After all, you had no dinner!"

"Nothing," he said. "Nothing! You get home. They may be telephoning—Bob or Johnnie, or somebody— and you might reassure 'em. I'll be along right away."

Hilary left the schoolhouse and found Cass searching for the car. The fire had died down now, and the line of watchers, silhouetted against the dull, red wall of its embers, was smaller now.

Underfoot were freezing pools of ashy water and slush. The landmarks of what a few hours earlier had been a peaceful street were obliterated. New vistas were opened by the engines' searchlights over smoking ruins, and the shrill voices of wide-awake children and excited women commented on the fact that you could see clear through to the foundries; you could see the oak trees clear over by the old bridge.

"I've got a couple of hens here," a stout old woman said loudly to anyone who would listen as she plowed among the throng. "Pore things, they was clean distracted. I'll keep 'em in my kitchen. I'm Mrs. Joe Clute—"

Hilary and Cass found the car, and Hilary climbed into the driver's seat. She wove her way through the confusion and was presently clear of the village and on her way up the hill. She stopped the car at the side door of the house and called to Abby, who had opened it, that the worst was over.

Then close beside her, somewhere in the darkness of the car, a child's voice—half fretful and half alarmed—called out: "Mother!" Another baby voice joined immediately in a crying wail. Hilary, frozen for a moment into deathlike rigidity, felt her heart begin to beat fast again, and twisted about to lean over the back seat, stretching down a hand to investigate there.

"Who—why, baby! What's the matter? Who are you? Don't cry, dear! I've got her, Abby! It's a little girl—it's Gemma Patroni—isn't that who you are, darling? And you—are you the little Harris boy? *Abby, we've found them!* And they're freezing—they're shaking. . . . How did you get into the car, and didn't you know your fathers were looking everywhere for you? Pick him up; I'll carry her, and we'll telephone Mr. Bridges at once! Ella," said Hilary to the startled older maid in the hall, "we've two frozen babies here. Run down and get them something to eat! No, I'll carry her. We've got to get them into blankets or they'll be ill."

The weight of the drowsy child was sweet in her strong arms as she mounted the stairs.

* * *

It was almost midnight when Jim came in but his wife was still reading, and she called to him to come into her room. He found her propped up on pillows, a smile in her eyes.

"Ah, you poor thing; you looked wrecked!" she said.

Jim dropped into a chair. "It's been pretty strenuous. So the lost kids were asleep in the back of the car?"

"Yes. They'd crawled in, and they were just about frozen. I'd have taken them back, but I didn't know where the Harris boy's mother was, and poor Mrs. Patroni is in the hospital with a new baby. You got messages to them?"

"Oh, yes. And where are the kids now?"

"Asleep."

"Up—?" He jerked his head backward.

Hilary's face paled a little, but she answered naturally enough. "Yes. In the nursery. Jim, are you starving?"

"Well, I was sort of wondering if Linda or Ella was around—anybody to get me a sandwich—"

"*I'm* around!" Hilary brought her feet to the floor, caught up a robe and tied it firmly about her. "I'll find you something," she said.

"Now liste—I don't want to bother you—"

"Jim, you're cold! Never mind; food will fix it!"

They switched on lights as they went cautiously downstairs, hand in hand, to find the great kitchen warm and orderly, and the icebox ready for them. Before long they were seated, ravenous, at the table, and Hilary had the satisfaction of seeing more than one cupful of hot coffee eagerly drunk, and a rested look come over her husband's dirty face under the disorderly mop of his hair.

"Jim, I never saw you look so filthy!"

"You had time for a bath."

"I got the children to bed first. And by that time, believe me, I needed it! The little girl can't be more than 3; and we spooned some milk toast into her, just to stave off chill. The boy is a darling—5, I should think, and as quick as a little fox."

"Our ages," he said with a great sigh.

"Yes, Daffy and Peter's ages," she agreed quietly. And then with resolution, her elbows on the table, her chin in her hands, she said, "Jim, I think I've made a great discovery tonight."

"So have I—I've discovered a cook," he smiled. "I don't think you've cooked me a meal since we went up into Canada and camped on our first anniversary."

When I first knew Peter was coming, her heart said. Aloud, she continued, "This is the discovery, Jim: That all children—*all* children"—her voice thickened, but she did not move her steady gaze from his—"are my children. All children are mine. Little, soft, drowsy things, needing to be fed and warmed and tucked down in bed. And that—that the world is full of children, Jim, so that I need never be—be childless again.

"She felt just like Daffy while I was undressing her and comforting her," Hilary went on when the man did not speak. "She put her little arms up to kiss me goodnight. And she dropped down into the crib with that long sigh, like Daffy, and was off. He stood—the boy stood—braced on his little firm legs, like our Peter, and orated to me (just like Peter!): 'I guess you'd think that was a pretty big fire, 'cause you're a girl! But I wasn't afraid!'

"Jim, as long as there are babies in the world who need mothering, I have a job. And this big house has a job, and the gardens, and the swimming pool. Once

English mothers came to find this country for the children's sake. Now it belongs to all the children of the world, for their sakes, for what they did. Don't you see? That's America's new job, to show them that they can all live together and be friends in spite of old national ties, in spite of religious differences—Morettis and Ranovitches and Silvas and Grogans and Harrises and Bernsteins and Hagopians—that's what they bought and paid for, those old first Americans!"

"But Hilary," he said, stirred as he was seldom stirred, and speaking with a tenderness of pity quite new to him, "you can't keep these youngsters, dear. They have mothers and fathers."

"Ah, but I don't mean *these*! I mean children who have been scared out of Europe by horrors that children ought never to know—or anyone else, for that matter! I mean girls and boys who don't know anything about us, whom we could keep happy—with a safe nursery for them, Jim, and toys and picnics and—and love."

"You think only two?" he asked, as she paused.

Tears rushed to her eyes, but she was smiling. "Ten, if you would," she said. "Twenty."

"For Daffy and Peter."

"For Daffy and Peter. And if we did, Jim, and had a crowd of happy, noisy, sturdy youngsters here—oh, not adopted, nothing hard or final about it, then mustn't they—and their parents, too—think kindly of us, through all the changes of history, and perhaps get the American idea of not hating anyone just because he happens to be of another race?

"It came to me tonight," Hilary went on, as Jim watched her with a half smile, a new look in his eyes, "that that scene—the scene at the fire on Christmas Eve—was American. All the races, all the names, united in a great effort to save the children, not to let the children be hurt or frightened! They're not like that in other countries, Jim. The children don't come first.

"But here they do. And when I saw the women comforting one another, starting to set up beds and wrap babies in blankets and get coffee pots boiling, I felt—I felt part of it, part of something much bigger than myself—part of what this generation of women has to do for America. And your share and mine is those children Middleton wrote you about!"

"You might be bitterly disappointed in them. They might be unfortunate children—slum children—" he interrupted reluctantly.

"Ah, but all the better! We've done away with slums at Bridgeover; we've been praised as the most modern of all the textile mills. Now we can extend it; we can mother and father so much more than a boy growing up to be rich, and a girl to be a debutante."

"We will!" he said suddenly, setting down his cup. "I'll go down to New York tomorrow and see Middleton. You'll have to come with me, and we'll send home beds and tables—whatever you'll need. Abby'll find us a couple of women to be nurses, and the Bridgeover International Nursery will get under way."

Hilary laughed brokenly, covering her face with her hands, and he left his chair and came around the table and knelt down beside her, taking her hands away, locking an arm around her waist. She managed to crook an arm about his neck.

"Jim, you are filthy, and you smell of smoke!" Hilary

murmured. It was his wife back again, after the long months, but a new wife, too, closer, dearer. He rubbed his chin against hers.

"And you smell so sweet—and you are so sweet!" he said.

"I'm so grateful—so grateful that you see it as I do!"

"Just to be able to do it is a great privilege," the man said soberly.

"Ah, Jim, we still have so much to be thankful for!"

"You," he said, smiling.

She countered, *"You!"* And then in a dreamy tone she added, "And if someday a Bridges baby comes along, why he'll find a houseful of friends ready to spoil him—" She stopped.

"But you said—" the man began, on a stupefied note.

"Yes, I know what I said. I was afraid! We'd been so sure of them—we'd been so proud. But now, when I can have 20 children—40 children—and give them a chance, why, one more little baby doesn't seem so unattainable, so terrifyingly precious."

"But the doctor—"

"Oh yes, Dr. Weeks said that in the nervous con-dition I was in it wouldn't be advisable. *Advisable!* I know when a thing's advisable or not, I hope! Ah, Jim, you don't know how much I want to be busy in the next two years."

"You lift me! My wife," he said. "I think I never knew you until now. The world begins again for us, Hilary. We've been takers. Now we begin as givers."

"I love you," she said, her lips against his cheek.

Jim didn't answer, but he tightened his arm, and she felt his forehead rest against her hair. And so they clung together for a few minutes that to them both were a glimpse of paradise regained.

Then Jim stirred and raised his hand, tipping his head to one side. "Listen!" he said. "Bells! It's the bells from the village. Christmas morning, Hilary. Merry Christmas, dear!"

"Oh, better than that," she replied. "We've grown up. Something older, wiser, and stronger than just being 'merry,' Jim. Perhaps we'll never be merry in the old way again. We belong to the world now, all the world, not just our own safe, rich little corner. And it's a long job to make the world happy, but we've found something better. We've found peace this Christmas!"

Christmas Carol

Margaret E. Sangster, Jr.

Sara hated her job. Life was so unfair!
Her listening mother, concerned, made a suggestion.
Just suppose—just pretending, of course—that she . . .

Sara Kimberly went on coloring cards. She thought: *Will I do this for the rest of my life, I wonder?* She painted a holly wreath (which should, by all means, have been bright green and red) a drab olive green. She thought: *I hate to put the finishing touches on another person's poor work!*

Sara's mother, sewing by the window, must have felt the oppressive quality of her daughter's thoughts. She looked up briefly from her sewing and spoke. "A penny for them, dear," she said.

Sara answered bitterly, "What I'm thinking wouldn't be worth a penny. I'm merely hating my job, as usual."

"Don't hate it, my dear," Mrs. Kimberly replied softly. "Hating one's task only makes that task seem harder. If you could try to enjoy your—"

"Enjoy!" Sara exclaimed. "If you had to color six dozen cheap cards a day when your whole soul is longing to sit before an easel in an art school and learn to paint real pictures, you wouldn't speak of enjoyment!"

Mrs. Kimberly sighed. She sewed steadily for several moments upon the shabby garment she was mending. Finally she said, "Why don't you make a game of it, Sara? Maybe that would help a bit. Don't think of the cards as work."

"What do you mean?" Sara asked, dipping her brush in the paint.

Mrs. Kimberly finished the garment she was mending and laid it aside then took up a stocking that was past its first youth. "It's nearly Christmas time. The whole world is glowing with happiness. Back home in the country, folks are thinking of hemlock trees and Yule logs. They're already beginning to plan the details of their holiday dinners. We mustn't forget the meaning of Christmas, dear, even though we live in a furnished room on a dingy city street."

Sara asked, "How can we keep from forgetting it? Surrounded by these monotonous gift cards, the meaning of Christmas seems rather lost to me."

Mrs. Kimberly spoke in an eager voice. "I've an idea, Sara, that will answer your question and solve your problem. As I suggested before, let's play a game with your greeting cards. Let's keep them from being ugly. Let's pretend that every single card you paint is a decoration we're placing in a home that we actually own. Let's make the six dozen cards you send out today a veritable Christmas carol."

Sara looked at her mother with an unpleasant quirk on what was, ordinarily, a pretty mouth. But the sight of her parent bending patiently above a chore of darning transformed the expression into a grudging smile.

"All right, Mommy," she said. "I'll stop being bitter. I won't make ugliness uglier than it is. I'll go you one better in this game you've invented: I'll pretend that I'm in art school, working on my own compositions. And I'll try to create cards that will hold at least a hint of the holiday spirit."

Hand coloring for a cheap gift-card house! Sara hadn't always done such work. Indeed, she had planned an intensive artistic career not much more than a year before. But then had come disaster cloaked in a bank failure and the foreclosure of her widowed mother's home, and Sara found herself bereft of a career and looking for employment. She and her mother had taken a furnished room in a nearby city, and she had begun to search the advertising columns and the help wanted sections of the daily newspapers. The search eventually had borne fruit, oddly enough in the shape of greeting cards to be colored. And Sara, accepting the work gratefully, still couldn't help feeling that it was a mockery of her heart's desire. The feeling grew as the weeks rolled into months, and only financial necessity, at last, kept her constantly at the coloring.

Spurred on by her mother's gallantry, Sara surveyed the next card on the unfinished pile. Why should she set her mind on hatred? Hating her work wouldn't get it done any faster! Why not make the best of a dull job? She took up the card and stared at its clumsy printed wreath. Ordinarily, she would have dabbed the wreath with color, hit or miss—anything to get by. But now, faintly intrigued by her mother's suggested game, she tried to visualize the wreath

hanging in a wide curtained window. She dipped her brush into a rich green, added a bow of gold, and lo! The wreath lost its clumsiness and became a charming bit of Christmas color.

The next card pictured a stiffly stuffed stocking, dangling against an unreal fireplace. A stupid card, done in a stupid fashion, but the vividness of scarlet paint, with the black stocking standing out in relief, transformed it. Warming to her work, Sara made that stocking an exciting affair. She filled it to overflowing with gifts of various shades.

Six dozen cards! They had seemed hopeless and endless when Sara began them. But as the fascination of the game grew upon her, they took on the luster of an adventure. Her mother put aside the mending basket to watch, and her words of applause were as spontaneously delighted as a happy child's. "What a holiday house we'll have!" Mrs. Kimberly kept murmuring. "What a glorious home!" And when the last of the six dozen cards had been completed, she said, "This has been our happiest time since we left the country. I can hardly wait, darling, for you to do tomorrow's cards."

There was a ring of sincerity in Sara's voice as she answered, "Neither can I!"

The snub-nosed office boy, who brought the cards in the morning and came for them in the late afternoon, arrived as Sara tied her day's work into a parcel. "Say, those are swell!" he said admiringly. "I'll come early tomorrow with the new batch." And he left, grinning over a homemade ginger cookie that Mrs. Kimberly had pressed into his hand.

After he had gone, Sara began to tidy the room, putting aside her paints and cleaning her brushes. As she did so, she resolutely put aside the thoughts of an art education that had for a year been haunting her. "I'll forget about the might-have-been and concentrate on the now," she told her mother as they shared a simple supper.

Her mother's eyes were misty as she applauded, "That's my brave girl!"

When Sara went to sleep that night, her last waking vision was of an amazingly beautiful Christmas tree. She drifted into sleep with the rhythm of merry sleigh bells in her brain. She woke to a glorious blue-and-white winter day and got out her paints and brushes with a feeling of anticipation that was almost akin to rapture.

"I hope the boy was telling the truth when he said he'd come early," she murmured, glancing at the clock. "I'm really anxious, Mommy, to go on with the game."

It was 9:00. At 9:30 Sara was standing by the window, waiting for the snub-nosed little messenger. At 10:30 she was still waiting. At 11:00 she turned away from the window.

"Something's happened," she said despairingly. "Maybe they've got another girl to do the work—and we need the money so badly. Maybe—"

"Don't cross bridges until you come to them, dear," Her mother said. "Probably the messenger boy didn't get in today. Perhaps he's ill, or on another errand."

But when noon came and still no messenger, Mrs. Kimberly was forced to share her daughter's apprehension. "Why don't you go to the office of the card company and ask what's happened?" she suggested. "It will be better than waiting like this."

Her feet winged with nervousness, Sara flew to the screened-off corner of the room doing double duty as a dressing room. That was how she missed seeing the car that drove up to the door, and the imposing gentleman who alighted from it and strode up the steps of the rooming house. She was standing, her hand on the doorknob, ready to leave, when emphatic fingers beat a sharp tattoo upon the door's outer panel.

At first sight, Sara and her mother thought that the opulent-looking gentleman must be a banker. He had the sort of appearance that is associated with money. But his second sentence dispelled the illusion. "Are you Miss Sara Kimberly?" and at Sara's word of affirmation, he continued. "I'm the owner of the Acme Greeting Card Company. My name is Jasper, Clarke Jasper."

"Mother, this is Mr. Jasper," Sara said, stepping away from the door "Do come in and sit down, Mr. Jasper, and—"

"—and tell you what this is all about?" finished the owner of the greeting card company.

As Sara and her mother leaned forward with rapt attention, Mr. Jasper told how that morning, though it was not his custom, he had checked over a stack of finished cards that had come in from a color artist.

"I was completely charmed by the radiance of color the artist had given to dull subject matter," he told Sara and her mother. "I thought, *It's too bad the drawings aren't of equal value.* And then this idea came to me in a flash. *I'll look up the person who did the coloring and find out what's back of her gift.* So I got your name from my office manager and started forth on a quest."

Sara wasn't an outspoken girl. She usually kept her dreams from strangers. But this man's kindly questions somehow unlocked the floodgates of her reticence. Almost without her own volition, she found herself telling the story of the country home that had been foreclosed on, the bank that had crashed, and the career that had gone a-begging. Mr. Jasper listened attentively, nodding his head from time to time but making little comment. When the story was finished, he spoke.

"I thought it was something like that," he said.

Mrs. Kimberly, who had said little, made a nervous gesture with slim fingers. "Sara was worried," she said. "She was starting down to your place to see if you'd taken the card coloring job from her. She was afraid—"

Mr. Jasper interrupted. "No, sir! Miss Sara Kimberly isn't, shall we say, "fired"—she's got a new job instead. From this moment on she's going to design cards for us, cards worthy to wear her colors. And two days a week she's going to have time off to attend art school at the expense of the company. No"—Mr. Jasper's hand was raised in protest—"don't thank me. I'm a solid business man, and I'm doing this for the good of the firm. If I can promote a genius, I'll expect her to stand by us, to give us some of her work in the years to come."

An hour after Mr. Jasper's departure, Sara and her mother were still sitting in their chairs, staring at each other. They weren't speaking; there wasn't much to say, really.

But between them, in that drab furnished room, there was a radiance of living light, the light of a renewed hope. And in their hearts a Christmas carol was making melody.

On Christmas Eve

Helen Stökl

She had been spoiled as a child, courted for her money by throngs of suitors, and married for love. But she was jealous of her artist husband, and even more jealous for the love of their little son.

Then came that tragic day when—oh, how could she re-live that terrible moment and what she'd said to her husband afterward?

It was the day before Christmas. In a railroad train, which was speeding from the capital city into the country and toward the mountains, sat a pale young woman. With dry, burning eyes she stared out upon the wintry fields over which swept the sharp wind, playfully driving a few solitary snowflakes before it. Like the snowflakes, her happiness had been blown and scattered. Once she had intended to hold it so securely; how had it been smashed to pieces in her hand? Before her mind's eye, pictures of the past rose slowly, one after the other.

She saw herself growing up in the house of her father, a rich old merchant. Surrounded by luxury and spoiled by flattery, she had been poor in the midst of her riches because no mother had watched over her.

She saw herself, scarcely arrived at maturity, sur-rounded by a throng of suitors, contending for the hand of the rich heiress. She had remained cold and indiffer-ent to every attention until there had stepped into her circle one, who with the first glance of his sunny, happy eyes, had taken unopposed possession of her being. But however high public opinion had placed the young painter whom her heart had chosen, he was not the sort of husband her father had wished for her. He didn't op-pose his daughter's passionate, impetuous will, but when she followed her beloved into his house as his wife, she couldn't escape the conviction that in win-ning a husband she had lost a father.

It grieved her, but what sacrifice would she not have made for her darling! The more she gave up for his sake, the more ardently he would love her. If she had no one but him, he must be everything to her. She had given him her young heart, whole and undivided. She expected his heart, whole and undivided, in return. She didn't know that the heart of a man—of an artist, in particular—cannot be filled simply and solely by a woman, though she be most beloved; that he has—and must have—in his life, other interests, other goals than her love. And when the recognition of this finally dawned upon her she didn't want to acknowledge it. She began to be jealous of everything that drew him from her—her friends, his art, his joyful outlook on life, and, at last, even their child.

She had realized with proud joy that the son she presented to him doubled her claim to his love, but this joy didn't long remain untroubled. The child was the exact image of his father. And as he had inherited the color of his hair and eyes, the sound of his voice, and his manner of smiling, so the child seemed to be nowhere happier than in the presence of his father. From the very arms of his mother he was always struggling toward his father. No sooner was he able to walk than he followed his father's every step, or sat patiently on the stairs to await his return. "Who do you love better, Daddy or Mommy?" she asked with trembling heart, when she was alone with the child. "Both—and then Daddy," answered the child, looking at her brightly with his big, honest eyes.

Vainly, she tried to make the child exclusively her own. The sunny, steadfast friendliness of the father exerted a stronger force of attraction than the passionate, agitated tenderness of the mother. *They are enough for each other; they don't need me!* was the tormenting thought she couldn't get rid of. Her health began to suffer.

"You are sick. The winter has been too long and difficult for you," said her husband, looking anxiously at her pale cheeks. "Let's go to the mountains; you'll soon feel better there."

She accepted the proposal eagerly. To get away into the mountains, perhaps it would be better there.

Imbedded deep in a narrow valley, accessible from only one direction, the mountain village they sought, was a retreat as romantic as it was peacefully quiet. It was the same village in which her husband, as a young, carefree artist, had spent several summers before his marriage. With the memory of former times, the old wanderlust came over him again. He wandered for days among the mountains, filling his sketchbook wherever occasion demanded, and putting up for the night wherever chance led him.

Several times she accompanied him on these sketching trips, but her restless nature wouldn't allow her to sit for hours while he, engrossed in his work, never gave her a glance. She remained at home, and the child went in her place. Leading him carefully by the hand over the steep places, or carrying him in his arms when his little legs were tired, the man took the boy to the place where he was working. Playing with stones and flowers, the child waited patiently and contentedly until the father had time to turn to him again. They were too happy on these walks together for it not to have been a torment to her.

"Leave the child here," she said, the next time he wanted to take him along.

"But why?"

"You can't keep your eyes on him while you're painting. He might come to some harm in the mountains."

"Why, the idea!" He burst out laughing. "He never leaves my side!"

"Just the same, I don't want him to go." She saw his surprised look and added passionately, "He's my child, as well as yours. Or do you want to take my child's love from me, too?"

He shrugged his shoulders and turned away, but he didn't take the child with him anymore.

And then came the end. With what uncanny clarity each detail of that horrible day came back to her! It was a Sunday. In the secret hope that he would stay with her that day, she had dressed herself with special care. "I'm going to church. Do you want to come with me?" she asked timidly.

"Not today. I want to finish the sketch from Red Wall Mountain, and I can use only morning light."

She turned away without a word.

"Are you going to take the child with you?" he asked.

"No, he'll stay here with the maid."

"Do you think it's safe to leave him in the care of such a young thing, who is only a child herself?"

"Why not? She has nothing else to do; she'll be able to take care of him."

He made no further objections, and she left. The church was at the far end of the village, and more than two hours passed before she returned. "Where is the child?" she asked the maid who stood before her, timid and embarrassed.

"He went with his father," the girl stammered. "I just ran across the street for a minute, and when I came back they were both gone."

So in spite of everything! She pressed her lips tightly together. Against her expressed wishes, in open defiance and derision of her, he had taken the child with him. Had it come to such a pass? She waited in feverish impatience.

Noon came, and they were still out. She took her hat and went to meet them. They could only come this way, and there they were coming, even now! A little procession of boy and man, her husband in the lead. But was it her husband? Without a hat, his clothes hanging in tatters, blood from a wound on his forehead falling in large drops upon the child in his arms . . . And the child! What was the matter with the child? Why was he lying so motionless? And why did he let his head hang so limply over his father's arm?

She was unable to take a step forward. Her teeth chattered as in a chill, while a convulsion shook her limbs and the cold sweat stood out on her brow.

Now her husband stood before her. "My child! My child!" The words came gasping from her breast. She wanted to speak, but she could not. With quivering lips she bent over the child who lay pale and staring in his father's arms. Everything glittered and swam before her eyes. Only indistinctly, as from a distance, came the murmurs of the bystanders: "He fell off Red Wall." Then, with a piercing cry, she collapsed in the dust of the road.

* * *

When she had been brought to the house, they succeeded in arousing her from her unconsciousness but not from the deep apathy that had taken possession of her. Indifferently, she looked on as they undressed the dead child and clothed him in his little white shroud, as they laid him in his coffin and covered him with flowers. No tears came to her eyes. Silent and self-absorbed she sat. When her husband tried to approach her, she turned away shuddering.

When the time for the funeral came, she pulled herself together. Without taking her husband's arm, she walked, silent and gloomy, behind the little coffin, saw it laid to rest in the earth, and the saw ground heaped over it.

Now the gravedigger had finished; the people, who had come out of curiosity or sympathy, had all dispersed; and she was left alone with her husband by the grave. With warm compassion he reached his hand toward her. "Why do you want to bear your sorrow alone, Anna?" he asked, his voice trembling with emotion. "Don't I suffer, too? Is it not the child of both of us whom we have buried here?"

She rejected his hand. "You no longer have any part in the child," she said dully.

"Anna!" he cried, frightened.

"You are guilty of his death," she continued with forced calmness. "In order to hurt me, to torture me, you took the child with you, and his death was the result. There can be no reconciliation for us over this grave."

"You say that I am guilty of the child's death? I am not! Listen to me—"

She interrupted him with passionate vehemence. "And even if you weren't, what difference could it make, since the love between us has long been dead!"

"Anna, Anna! You don't know what you're saying!"

"I know only too well. You have long since ceased to love me, even if I still cared for you, and I don't love you, either. Our paths go different ways."

"You are beside yourself. When you are calmer you will think differently."

"Never!" she cried, quivering with passion. "Haven't I told you that I no longer love you, that I have long since ceased to love you? Will you compel me to live at your side with a heart that hates you? If it is my inheritance you are thinking of—"

He straightened up and strode away without once looking around.

That same evening he returned to the capital. When she followed a few days later, he was no longer there. He had left a letter for her that contained the necessary arrangements to put her again in sole possession of her inheritance, and also directed her to a lawyer who was authorized by him to grant her a divorce as soon as she wanted it. He himself had gone on a trip.

Nearly three years passed, and she had not seen him again. From time to time she read a notice in the papers of a new picture he had painted, or she saw one herself in some exhibition. That was all.

She had not remained at home, either. Her health seriously affected, she spent her winters in Nice, and her summers at various watering places. She had never asked for the divorce; she had no use for freedom. What would she have done with it?

This was the first winter she had spent in her own country again. So long as she remained abroad, it was comparatively easy to shut out the thoughts she didn't want to think. Now, at home again among the old surroundings, everything was a powerful reminder of the past. In order to escape from herself she tried to occupy her time with charitable activities. Her heart had always beat with warm sympathy for the poor and needy. For some time she had succeeded in forgetting herself in concern for others. In the midst of the preparations for the Christmas festivities, however, her strength failed her. The memory of her former happiness assailed her with a power from which there was no escape.

How blissfully she once had celebrated Christmas with her husband and her child! Every thought of the past was soured and embittered for her. Only the memory of Christmas shone forth bright and radiant out of the darkness.

Suddenly it came over her with irresistible longing: she wanted to go to her child! She wanted to kneel beside his grave at Christmas. Perhaps there comfort would come into her tired, despairing heart. So she left behind rich presents for her protegés among the poor, and on the morning of Christmas Eve she was traveling, quite alone, to the mountains and the quiet village where she would visit her child.

The train reached the last station on the branch line, and she got out. It was still a half hour's walk to the village, but she need not go to the village itself. The cemetery was situated by itself, somewhat apart, on the slope of the mountain. She was glad that it was so. It would have seemed unbearable to her to be stared at, questioned, or even accompanied to the cemetery. No, she wanted to be there alone, quite alone with her child.

Faster and faster she walked. Then she stood, gasping for breath, before the churchyard gate. She pressed on the latch, but the gate was locked. However obvious the thought that the lonely cemetery would not be left open, especially in winter, the possibility had not occurred to her. She looked around. Would she have to go to the village, after all, and arouse the curiosity of its inhabitants?

Then her glance fell on a little house that stood a few hundred yards away on the mountainside. She remembered having heard that a woodcutter lived there with his family. The man, whose work kept him in the mountains for weeks at a time, would scarcely know her. And what if he did?

She went to the house. The gate was unlocked, and she groped her way along a dark, narrow path to the door. The noise that forced its way out through the door made knocking seem a futile gesture. She opened the door gently and looked into the room. Near a large wooden table in the center sat an old, gray-haired man, earnestly intent on feeding porridge to a baby clasped firmly between his knees. With the touchingly diligent movements that men always make when they do women's work, he dipped the spoon in the porridge, blew on it, carried it cautiously to his own lips, and then to the greedily gaping mouth of the child. He spoke soothingly to the infant when, from time to time, he carried the full spoon past it and into the mouth of a plump-cheeked youngster who stood next to him. A number of older children romped noisily about the room, and one girl, perhaps 11 years old, sat quietly knitting by the window.

As his glance fell on the strange woman who stood hesitating on the doorstep, he tried to stand up with the child. She quickly motioned him to remain seated.

"I want to get into the cemetery, but it is locked. Have you anyone you could send to the village to get the key for me?"

"You want the key to the cemetery? Why, sure! Tony can get it for you in no time. Go on, Tony," he said to a half-grown lad, who had curiously come forward with the other children. "Run to the village for the key—and be quick about it, do you hear?"

The boy snatched his cap and rushed out.

"Won't you sit down, ma'am? Nellie, bring a chair. My daughter has gone to the village to buy bread for the holiday, and my son hasn't come home from work yet, so Grandpa has to play nursemaid, whether he wants to or not."

"Are these all your grandchildren?" asked the young woman, looking around the room with interest.

"Yes, indeed! Seven of 'em, all healthy and with good appetites. Hey, Frankie, where do you think you're going? To meet Daddy? What they don't think of! Stay here, or Santa Claus won't bring you anything. Those children hang on their father like burrs—always want to be with him. In the summer I can't keep them from sneaking off and chasing after him when he goes to work. He likes it, you know, but I don't allow it. Ever since the time I saw a summer visitor's little boy lying dead before me who had fallen because he ran secretly after his father. I don't have any peace unless I know the children are with me."

The young woman had suddenly grown pale, but the old man, who was shifting the child to a more comfortable position in his lap, didn't notice it.

"What child was that?" she asked urgently.

"Didn't you ever hear about the little boy who fell to his death from Red Wall? It happened three years ago this summer."

"Do you mean the son of the painter who was here at that time?" The young woman's voice trembled slightly "But that child didn't run after his father. The father took him along, and then let him fall through negligence."

"That isn't so!" cried the old man earnestly. "That's what people said because the maid, who was supposed to look after him, told that story in her distress at having left the child alone. But I was there—I know how it happened."

"You were *there?*" The young woman turned her big, staring eyes upon him.

"Certainly I was there! Would you like to hear how it happened? It was on a Sunday. I had just come from church, and as I was passing Red Wall I saw the visiting gentleman sitting there painting, and because he usually had his little boy with him, I went up to him and said, 'Where's the little fellow today, if I may ask?'

"'The little fellow?' he said, laughing. 'Oh, yes! I had to leave him at home today. My wife won't let him go with me. She's afraid something might happen to him in the mountains.'

"I was just about to say, 'Your wife is right,' when he jumped up beside me. 'Didn't you hear anything?' he asked. It had seemed to me, too, as if someone had called, and as we stood perfectly still we heard it again quite clearly. 'Daddy! Daddy!' We looked all around, and then up above, for it seemed as if the voice came out of the air! And as we looked up at the Wall, sure enough, there was the boy! Just overhead, with his little hands clinging to the bushes and his little feet braced against the cliff. He was hanging directly over the precipice and calling in his shrill voice, 'Daddy, Daddy, I was trying to find you, but I slipped down here and I can't get up again. You'll have to get me!'

"The man's face became white as chalk. For a moment he was unable to speak. Then, with an effort, he called quite calmly, in order not to frighten the child: 'I'm coming, Charlie! Just hold on tight, good and tight, do you hear? I'll be right with you!'

"With huge strides he dashed up the side of the mountain, through the thickets, and before I would have thought it possible, he was there. Cautiously, he knelt down and leaned over the edge, but he couldn't reach the child with his hand.

"'Hold on just a minute longer, Charlie,' he called. 'I'm going to get a stick.' But when the child saw him so suddenly above him, he shouted for joy and let go with one hand in order to grab his father. The other hand couldn't support his weight and his feet slipped on the smooth rock. 'Daddy! Daddy! Hold me!' he cried. And then he fell. From down below, I couldn't see where he landed, but I heard him hit the rocks.

"I hurried up the mountain as fast as I could, but the father was already coming toward me. He hadn't been able to get to the child from above; now he tried from the side, and from below. It was useless. So he ran to the next woodcutter's camp to get help. The people brought a rope back with them, and the father tied it around himself. He wouldn't let anyone else go after the child. I was standing near when they pulled him up again. The rope had twisted, and his head had been thrown against the cliff so that the blood ran all over his forehead, but he had taken care that the child had not struck anywhere. 'He isn't dead; he's only stunned,' he insisted. But from the way the limbs hung down so limply, I knew the child's back was broken, and he was past help. The father must have realized it himself when he got to the top. Without a word, he pushed away the people who wanted to carry the child for him. He gathered the boy up in his arms and climbed down with him to the village. I didn't go with him; I couldn't bear the sight."

The old man passed his coat sleeve over his eyes. When he looked up again he saw the young woman, deathly pale, sunk back in her chair. "Nellie! Nellie!" he called, frightened. "A glass of water, quickly! The lady isn't feeling well."

She drank eagerly of the offered water. "It's just the heat in the room," she stammered, trying hard to compose herself.

"Yes, it is hot here," agreed the old man. "But thank goodness, here's Tony now. Do you want him to go with you so he can bring the key back?"

"No, no. I'll bring it back myself." She drew her cloak around her and hurried to the cemetery.

For some time her trembling hands tried vainly to open the lock, and at last she was successful. How lonely but how peaceful the rows of graves lay under their thin, uniform blankets of snow! Her glance roamed searchingly about. Yes, there it was. Close beside a grave sheltered by towering pines was the little cross that she had sent from the city to mark her child's resting place, and which bore no other inscription than his name and the date of his death.

With a cry she rushed to the grave. All the dull misery that had lain upon her throughout the years, all the bitterness and sorrow that had piled up in her, all that she had ever kept back within herself now came forth in a violent outburst beside the little mound in which her child was resting for eternity. Embracing the grave in both her arms, her forehead pressed to the cold earth, she broke out into weeping so bitter, so convulsive, that her whole body swayed and trembled as if shaken by a storm.

She did not hear the creaking of the churchyard gate nor the footsteps approaching lightly over the snow. Suddenly she started up in fright. Had someone called her name? Half rising, her hand resting on the grave, she looked around, bewildered.

Directly opposite her, half concealed by the branches of the pines, stood a dark figure. She sprang up. Was she mistaken? Was it really her husband who stood before her, gazing at her earnestly and sadly?

"Richard!" she cried, coming forward in her first surprise as if to throw herself in his arms. But she recovered herself immediately. "How did you get here?" she asked, stepping back.

"Just as you did, driven by the desire to see our child on Christmas Eve. I had no idea that you would be here or I would have come later. However, I can leave if I am disturbing you," he added bitterly, when she didn't speak.

"Why should you disturb me?" she said softly, without looking at him. "On the contrary, I'm glad you're here. I want to say something to you."

He leaned forward expectantly.

"I have just heard for the first time how our child died," she went on, hesitantly. "I was unjust when I blamed you for his death."

"You were," he replied in a hollow tone.

"Why didn't you correct me?"

"You wouldn't listen."

"You should have *made* me listen." She wrung her hands nervously. "You weren't guilty of his death. No! I killed him when I left such a giddy young girl in charge of him."

"Why do you make yourself miserable with such thoughts? I might just as well say if I had never taken the child with me it would never have occurred to him to run after me. God willed it so—and perhaps it is better for the child that he died."

The tone of his last words sounded so discouraged that she raised her eyes to him. How changed he was! She noticed it now for the first time. A deep crease was engraved between his eyes that had lost their sunny glance. The mouth had a bitter expression that she had never seen in him before. It cut her to the heart to see him thus.

"I made you very unhappy," she said softly.

"Did I make you happy? Neither of us knew how to care for the other's happiness."

"The fault was mine, not yours," she whispered almost inaudibly. "I wanted too much, and then to lose everything—" Hesitating, she looked down at the ground. Suppressing with difficulty the trembling in her voice, she asked, "This is Christmas Eve. Will you give me your hand over this little grave in token that you have forgiven me? I believe that we could then leave each other with lighter hearts."

He didn't answer. Anxiously she looked up. With heaving breast he stood before her. "Must we leave each other again?" the words squeezed slowly between his lips.

She looked at him as if she didn't understand. His eyes gazed fully and deeply into hers. And suddenly it came over her like a wave of fire. Was that not the old love light that she saw in his eyes, the light with which he had first wooed her, with which he had won her heart and made it happy thousands of times, and which she had never hoped to see again?

"Can't we get together again, Anna?" he asked, slowly reaching his arms out toward her.

Her knees refused to support her. She reeled, and would have fallen if he had not caught her in his arms.

"You can't love me any more," she faltered.

He laid her head gently on his breast and, kissing the tears from her eyes, he murmured, "I have never stopped loving you."

Suddenly through the deep stillness came the sound of the bells that heralded Christmas Eve in the nearby village. Beginning softly at first then growing ever louder and clearer, they filled the air with their jubilant, triumphant ringing. Overcome by a feeling of reverence, the couple stood still.

Touched in their innermost souls, they vowed that no other Christmas Eve should ever find them separated from their love but flooded and saturated with it. Then they walked, hand in hand, their glistening eyes raised to the starry heavens, over the lonely heath through the dark of the Holy Night, toward the dawn of their new life.

The Mansion

Henry Van Dyke

For 16 years I have held off including this story in one of our Christmas collections. Van Dyke's other great Christmas story, "The Other Wise Man," was featured in Christmas in My Heart 3.

"The Mansion" has had a seismic impact on my own spiritual journey. In fact, it is safe to say that no other non-biblical Christmas story even comes close, for it is that rarity—a life-changer. Though it may appear a bit archaic (it's 97 years old), once its message is fully internalized, the same message Christ, Saint Nicholas, and Lloyd C. Douglas preached, that one cannot receive credit for good works in two places at once, the reader's life can never be the same again.

There was an air of calm and reserved opulence about the Weightman mansion that spoke not of money squandered, but of wealth prudently applied. Standing on a corner of the avenue no longer fashionable for residence, it looked upon the swelling tide of business with an expression of complacency and half-disdain.

The house was not beautiful. There was nothing in its straight front of chocolate-colored stone, its heavy cornices, its broad staring windows of plate glass, its carved and bronze-bedecked mahogany doors at the top of the wide stoop, to charm the eye or fascinate the imagination. But it was eminently respectable and, in its way, imposing. It seemed to say that the glittering shops of the jewelers, the milliners, the confectioners, the florists, the picture dealers, the furriers, the makers of rare and costly antiquities, retail traders in luxuries of life, were beneath the notice of a house that had its foundations in high finance, and was built literally and figuratively in the shadow of St. Petronius' Church.

At the same time there was something self-pleased and congratulatory in the way in which the mansion held its own amid the changing neighborhood. It almost seemed to be lifted up a little among the tall buildings near at hand, as if it felt the rising value of the land on which it stood.

John Weightman was like the house he had built himself 30 years before and in which his ideals and ambitions were encrusted. He was a self-made man. But in making himself he had chosen a highly esteemed pattern and worked according to the approved rules. There was nothing irregular, questionable, or flamboyant about him. He was solid, correct, and justly successful.

His minor tastes, of course, had been carefully kept up to date. At the proper time, pictures by the Barbizon masters, old English plate and portraits, bronzes by Barye and marbles by Rodin, Persian carpets and Chinese porcelains, had been introduced to the mansion. It contained a Louis Quinze reception room, an Empire drawing room, a Jacobean dining room, and various apartments dimly reminiscent of the styles of furni-

101

ture affected by deceased monarchs. That the hallways were too short for the historic perspective did not make much difference. American decorative art is *capable de tout*, it absorbs all periods. Of each period Mr. Weightman wished to have something of the best. He understood its value, present as a certificate, and prospective as an investment.

It was only in the architecture of his town house that he remained conservative, immovable, one might almost say Early-Victorian-Christian. His country house at Dulwich-on-the-Sound was a palace of the Italian Renaissance. But in town he adhered to an architecture that had moral associations, the Nineteenth-Century-Brownstone epoch. It was a symbol of his social position, his religious doctrine, and even, in a way, of his business creed.

"A man of fixed principles," he would say, "should express them in the looks of his house. New York changes its domestic architecture too rapidly. It is like divorce. It is not dignified. I don't like it. Extravagance and fickleness are advertised in most of these new houses. I wish to be known for different qualities. Dignity and prudence are the things that people trust. Everyone knows that I can afford to live in the house that suits me. It is a guarantee to the public. It inspires confidence. It helps my influence. There is a text in the Bible about 'a house that hath foundations.' That is the proper kind of a mansion for a solid man."

Harold Weightman had often listened to his father discoursing in this fashion on the fundamental principles of life, and always with a divided mind. He admired immensely his father's talents and the single-minded energy with which he improved them. But in the paternal philosophy there was something that disquieted and oppressed the young man, and made him gasp inwardly for fresh air and free action.

At times, during his college course and his years at the law school, he had yielded to this impulse and broken away—now toward extravagance and dissipation, and then, when the reaction came, toward a romantic devotion to work among the poor. He had felt his father's disapproval for both of these forms of imprudence, but never in a harsh or violent way, always with a certain tolerant patience, such as one might show for the mistakes and vagaries of the very young. John Weightman was not hasty, impulsive, or inconsiderate, even toward his own children. With them, as with the rest of the world, he felt that he had a reputation to maintain, a theory to vindicate. He could afford to give them time to see that he was absolutely right.

One of his favorite Scripture quotations was "Wait on the Lord." He had applied it to real estate and to people, with profitable results.

But to human persons the sensation of being waited for is not always agreeable. Sometimes, especially with the young, it produces a vague restlessness, an inner resentment, which is increased by the fact that one can hardly explain or justify it. Of this John Weightman was not conscious. It lay beyond his horizon. He did not take it into account in the plan of life which he had made for himself and for his family as the sharers and inheritors of his success.

"Father plays us," said Harold, in a moment of irritation, to his mother, "like pieces in a game of chess."

"My dear," said that lady, whose faith in her husband was religious, "you ought not to speak so impatiently. At least he wins the game. He is one of the most respected men in New York. And he is very generous, too."

"I wish he would be more generous in letting us be ourselves," said the young man. "He always has something in view for us and expects to move us up to it."

"But isn't it always for our benefit?" replied his mother. "Look what a position we have! No one can say there is any taint on our money. There are no rumors about your father. He has kept the laws of God and of man. He has never made any mistakes."

Harold got up from his chair and poked the fire. Then he came back to the ample, well-gowned, firm-looking lady, and sat beside her on the sofa. He took her hand gently and looked at the two rings—a thin band of yellow gold, and a small solitaire diamond—which kept their place on her third finger in modest dignity, as if not shamed, but rather justified, by the splendor of the emerald which glittered beside them.

"Mother," he said, "you have a wonderful hand. And father made no mistake when he won you. But are you sure he has always been so inerrant?"

"Harold," she exclaimed, a little stiffly, "what do you mean? His life is an open book."

"Oh," he answered, "I don't mean anything bad, mother dear. I know the governor's life is an open book—a ledger, if you like, kept in the best bookkeeping hand, and always ready for inspection—every page correct, and showing a handsome balance. But isn't it a mistake not to let us make our own mistakes, to learn for ourselves, to live our own lives? Must we be always working for 'the balance,' in one thing or another? I want to be myself—to get outside of this everlasting, profitable 'plan'—to let myself go, and lose myself for a while at least, to do the things that I want to do just because I want to do them."

"My boy," said his mother, anxiously, "you are not going to do anything wrong or foolish? You know the falsehood of that old proverb about wild oats."

He threw back his head and laughed. "Yes, Mother," he answered, "I know it well enough. But in California, you know, the wild oats are one of the most valuable crops. They grow all over the hillsides and keep the cattle and the horses alive. But that isn't what I meant, to sow wild oats. Say to pick wild flowers, if you like, or even to chase wild geese. To do something that seems good to me just for its own sake, not for the sake of wages of one kind or another. I feel like a hired man, in the service of this magnificent mansion, in training for father's place as majordomo. I'd like to get out some way, to feel free, perhaps to do something for others."

The young man's voice hesitated a little. "Yes, it sounds like cant, I know, but sometimes I feel as if I'd like to do some good in the world, if Father only wouldn't insist upon God's putting it into the ledger."

His mother moved uneasily and a slight look of bewilderment came into her face. "Isn't that almost irreverent?" she asked. "Surely the righteous must have their reward. And your father is good. See how much he gives to all the established charities, how many things he has founded. He's always thinking of others, and planning for them. And surely, for us, he does everything. How well he has planned this trip to Europe for me and the girls—the court presentation at Berlin, the season on the Riviera, the visits in England with the Plumptons and the Halverstones. He says Lord Halverstone has the finest old house in Sussex, pure Elizabethan, and all the old customs are kept up, too—family prayers every morning for all the domestics. By the way, you know his son, Bertie, I believe."

Harold smiled a little to himself as he answered, "Yes, I fished at Catalina Island last June with the Honorable Ethelbert. He's rather a decent chap, in spite of his in-growing mind. But you, Mother; you are simply magnificent! You are Father's masterpiece." The young man leaned over to kiss her, and went up to the Riding Club for his afternoon canter in the Park.

* * *

So it came to pass, early in December, that Mrs. Weightman and her two daughters sailed for Europe on their serious pleasure trip, even as it had been written in the Book of Providence; and John Weightman, who had made the entry, was left to pass the rest of the winter with his son and heir in the brownstone mansion.

They were comfortable enough. The machinery of the massive establishment ran as smoothly as a great electric dynamo. They were busy enough, too. John Weightman's plans and enterprises were complicated, though his principle of action was always simple: to get good value for every expenditure and effort. The banking house of which he was the chief, the brain, the will, the absolutely controlling hand, was so admirably organized

that the details of its direction took but little time. But the scores of other interests that radiated from it and were dependent upon it (or, perhaps it would be more accurate to say, that contributed to its solidity and success), the many investments, industrial, political, benevolent, reformatory, ecclesiastical, that had made the name of Weightman well known and potent in city, church, and state, demanded much attention and careful steering in order that each might produce the desired result. There were board meetings of corporations and hospitals, conferences in Wall Street and at Albany, consultations and committee meetings in the brownstone mansion.

For a share in all this business and its adjuncts, John Weightman had his son in training in one of the famous law firms of the city; for he held that banking itself is a simple affair. The only real difficulties of finance are on its legal side. Meanwhile, he wished the young man to meet and know the men with whom he would have to deal when he became a partner in the house. So a couple of dinners were given in the mansion during December, after which the father called the son's attention to the fact that more than a hundred million* dollars had sat around the board.

But on Christmas Eve father and son were dining together without guests, and their talk across the broad table, glittering with silver and cut glass and softly lit by shaded candles, was intimate, though a little slow at times. The elder man was in rather a rare mood, more expansive and confidential than usual, and when the coffee was brought in and they were left alone, he talked more freely of his personal plans and hopes than he had ever done before.

"I feel very grateful tonight," said he, at last. "It must be something in the air of Christmas that gives me this feeling of thankfulness for the many divine mercies that have been bestowed upon me. All the principles by which I have tried to guide my life have been justified. I have never made the value of this salted almond by anything that the courts would not uphold, at least in the long run, and yet—or wouldn't it be truer to say and therefore?—my affairs have been wonderfully prospered. There's a great deal in that text 'Honesty is the best.' But no, that's not from the Bible, after all, is it? Wait a moment; there is something of that kind, I know."

"May I light a cigar, Father," said Harold, turning away to hide a smile, "while you are remembering the text?"

"Yes, certainly," answered the elder man, rather shortly. "You know I don't dislike the smell. But it is a wasteful, useless habit, and therefore I have never practiced it. Nothing useless is worthwhile, that's my motto—nothing that does not bring the reward. Oh, now I recall the text, 'Verily I say unto you, they have their reward.' I shall ask Doctor Snodgrass to preach a sermon on that verse some day."

"Using you as an illustration?"

"Well, not exactly that; but I could give him some good material from my own experience to prove the truth of Scripture. I can honestly say that there is not one of my charities that has not brought me in a good return, either in the increase of influence, the building up of credit, or the association with substantial people. Of course, you have to be careful how you give, in order to secure the best results—no indiscriminate giving, no pennies in beggars' hats! It has been one of my principles always to use the same kind of judgment in charities that I use in my other affairs, and they have not disappointed me."

"Even the check that you put in the plate when you take the offertory up the aisle on Sunday morning?"

"Certainly, though there the influence is less direct; and I must confess that I have my doubts in regard to the collection for foreign missions. That always seems to me romantic and wasteful. You never hear from it in any definite way. They say the missionaries have done a good deal to open the way for trade. Perhaps; but they have also gotten us into commercial and political difficulties. Yet I give to them a little. It is a matter of conscience with me to identify myself with all the enterprises of the church; it is the mainstay of social order and a prosperous civilization. But the best forms of benevolence are the well-established, organized ones here at home, where people can see them and know what they are doing."

"You mean the ones that have a local habitation and a name."

"Yes; they offer by far the safest return, though of course there is something gained by contributing to general funds. A public man can't afford to be without public spirit. But on the whole I prefer a building, or an endowment. There is a mutual advantage to a good name and a good institution in their connection in the public mind. It helps them both. Remember that, my boy. Of course, at the beginning you will have to practice it in a small way; later, you will have larger opportunities. But try to put your gifts where they can be identified and do good all around. You'll see the wisdom of it in the long run."

"I can see it already, sir, and the way you describe it

looks amazingly wise and prudent. In other words, we must cast our bread on the waters in large loaves, carried by sound ships marked with the owner's name, so that the return freight will be sure to come back to us."

The father laughed, but his eyes were frowning a little as if he suspected something irreverent under the respectful reply. "You put it humorously, but there's sense in what you say. Why not? God rules the sea, but He expects us to follow the laws of navigation and commerce. Why not take good care of your bread, even when you give it away?"

"It's not for me to say why not—and yet I can think of cases"—the young man hesitated for a moment. His half-finished cigar had gone out. He rose and tossed it into the fire, in front of which he remained standing—a slender, eager, restless young figure, with a touch of hunger in the fine face, strangely like and unlike the father, at whom he looked with half-wistful curiosity.

"The fact is, sir," he continued, "there is such a case in my mind right now, and it is a good deal on my heart, too. So I thought of speaking to you about it tonight. You remember Tom Rollins, the junior who was so good to me when I entered college?"

The father nodded. He remembered very well indeed the annoying incidents of his son's first escapade, and how Rollins had stood by him and helped to avoid a public disgrace, and how a close friendship had grown between the two boys, so different in their fortunes.

"Yes," he said, "I remember him. He was a promising young man. Has he succeeded?"

"Not exactly. That is, not yet. His business has been going rather badly. He has a wife and a little baby, you know. And now he has broken down with tuberculosis. The doctor says his only chance is a year or 18 months in Colorado. I wish we could help him."

"How much would it cost?"

"Three or four thousand perhaps, as a loan."

"Does the doctor say he will get well?"

"A fighting chance, the doctor says."

The face of the older man changed subtly. Not a line was altered, but it seemed to have a different substance, as if it were carved out of some firm, imperishable stuff.

"A fighting chance," he said, "may do for a speculation, but it is not a good investment. You owe something to young Rollins. Your grateful feeling does you credit. But don't overwork it. Send him three or four hundred, if you like. You'll never hear from it again, except in the letter of thanks. But, for heaven's sake, don't be sentimental. Religion is not a matter of sentiment; it's a matter of principle."

The face of the younger man changed now. But instead of becoming fixed and graven, it seemed to melt into life by the heat of an inward fire. His nostrils quivered with quick breath, his lips were curled.

"Principle!" he said. "You mean principal—and interest, too. Well, sir, you know best whether that is religion or not. But if it is, count me out, please. Tom saved me from going to the devil six years ago; and I'll be damned if I don't help him to the best of my ability now."

John Weightman looked at his son steadily. "Harold," he said at last, "you know I dislike violent language, and it never has any influence with me. If I could honestly approve of this proposition of yours, I'd let you have the money; but I can't. It's extravagant and useless. But you have your Christmas check for $1,000 coming to you to-morrow. You can use it as you please. I never interfere with your private affairs."

"Thank you," said Harold. "Thank you very much! But there's another private affair. I want to get away from this life, this town, this house. It stifles me. You refused last summer when I asked you to let me go up to Grenfell's Mission on the Labrador. I could go now, at least as far as the Newfoundland Station. Have you changed your mind?"

"Not at all. I think it is an exceedingly foolish enter-prise. It would interrupt the career that I have marked out for you."

"Well, then, here's a cheaper proposition. Algy Vanderhoof wants me to join him on his yacht with—well, with a little party—to cruise in the West Indies. Would you prefer that?"

"Certainly not! The Vanderhoof set is wild and god-less—I do not wish to see you keeping company with fools who walk in the broad and easy way that leads to perdi-tion."

"It is rather a hard choice," said the young man with a short laugh, turning toward the door. "According to you there's very little difference—a fool's paradise, or a fool's hell! Well, it's one or the other for me, and I'll toss up for it tonight: heads, I lose; tails, the devil wins. Anyway, I'm sick of this, and I'm out of it."

"Harold," said the older man (and there was a slight tremor in his voice), "don't let us quarrel on Christmas Eve. All I want is to persuade you to think seriously of the duties and responsibilities to which God has called you, so don't speak lightly of heaven and hell. Remember, there is another life."

The young man came back and laid his hand upon his father's shoulder. "Father," he said, "I want to remember it. I try to believe in it. But somehow or other, in this house it all seems unreal to me. No doubt all you say is perfectly right and wise. I don't venture to argue against it, but I can't feel it, that's all. If I'm to have a soul, either to lose or to save, I must really live. Just now, neither the present nor the future means anything to me. But surely we won't quarrel. I'm very grateful to you, and we'll part friends. Good night, sir."

The father held out his hand in silence. The heavy portiere dropped noiselessly behind the son, and he went up the wide, curving stairway to his own room.

Meanwhile, John Weightman sat in his carved chair in the Jacobean dining room. He felt strangely old and dull. The portraits of beautiful women by Lawrence and Reynolds and Raeburn, which had often seemed like real company to him, looked remote and uninteresting. He fancied something cold, and almost unfriendly, in their expression, as if they were staring through him, or beyond him. They cared nothing for his principles, his hopes, his disappointments, his successes. They belonged to another world in which he had no place. At this he felt a vague resentment, a sense of discomfort that he could not have defined or explained. He was used to being considered, re-spected, appreciated, at his full value in every region, even in that of his own dreams.

Presently he rang for the butler, telling him to close the house and not to sit up, and walked with lagging steps into the long library, where the shaded lamps were burn-ing. His eye fell upon the low shelves full of costly books,

but he had no desire to open them. Even the carefully chosen pictures that hung above them seemed to have lost their attraction. He paused for a moment before an idyll of Carot, a dance of nymphs around some forgotten altar in a vaporous glade, and looked at it curiously. There was something rapturous and serene about the picture—a breath of springtime in the misty trees, a harmony of joy in the dancing figures—that wakened in him a feeling of half-pleasure and half-envy. It represented something that he had never known in his calculated, orderly life. He was dimly mistrustful of it.

It is certainly very beautiful, he thought, *but it is distinctly pagan. That altar is built to some heathen god. It does not fit into the scheme of a Christian life. I doubt whether it is consistent with the tone of my house. I will sell it this winter. It will bring three or four times what I paid for it. That was a good purchase, a very good bargain.*

He dropped into the revolving chair before his big library table. It was covered with pamphlets and reports of the various enterprises in which he was interested. There was a pile of newspaper clippings in which his name was mentioned with praise for his sustaining power as a pillar of finance, for his judicious benevolence, for his support of wise and prudent reform movements, for his discretion in making permanent public gifts—"the Weightman Charities," one very complaisant editor called them, as if they deserved classification as a distinct species.

He turned the papers over listlessly. There was a description and a picture of the "Weightman Wing of the Hospital for Cripples," of which he was president; and an article on the new professor in the "Weightman Chair of Political Jurisprudence" in Jackson University, of which he was a trustee; and an illustrated account of the opening of the "Weightman Grammar School" at Dulwich-on-the-Sound, where he had his legal residence for purposes of taxation.

This last was perhaps the most carefully planned of all the Weightman Charities. He desired to win the confidence and support of his rural neighbors. It had pleased him much when the local newspaper had spoken of him as an ideal citizen and the logical candidate for the Governorship of the State; but upon the whole it seemed to him wiser to keep out of active politics. It would be easier and better to put Harold into the running and have him sent to the Legislature from the Dulwich district, then to the national House, then to the Senate. Why not? The Weightman interests were large enough to need a direct representative and guardian at Washington.

But tonight all these plans came back to him with dust upon them. They were dry and crumbling like forsaken habitations. The son, upon whom his honorable ambition had rested, had turned his back upon the mansion of his father's hopes. The break might not be final and, in any event, there would be much to live for; the fortunes of the family would be secure. But the zest of it all would be gone if John Weightman had to give up the assurance of perpetuating his name and his principles in his son. It was a bitter disappointment, and he felt that he had not deserved it.

He rose from the chair and paced the room with leaden feet. For the first time in his life his age was visibly upon him. His head was heavy and hot, and the thoughts that rolled in it were confused and depressing. Could it be that he had made a mistake in the principles of his existence? There was no argument in what Harold had said. It was almost childish—and yet it had shaken the elder man more deeply than he cared to show. It held a silent attack that touched him more than open criticism.

Suppose the end of his life were nearer than he thought (the end must come some time)—what if it were now? Had he not founded his house upon a rock? Had he not kept the Commandments? Was he not, "touching the law, blameless"? And beyond this, even if there were some faults in his character (and all men are sinners), yet he surely believed in the saving doctrines of religion: the forgiveness of sins, the resurrection of the body, the life everlasting. Yes, that was the true source of comfort, after all. He would read a bit in the Bible, as he did every night, and go to bed and to sleep.

He went back to his chair at the library table. A strange weight of weariness rested upon him, but he opened the book at a familiar place, and his eyes fell upon the verse at the bottom of the page.

"Lay not up for yourselves treasures upon earth."

That had been the text of the sermon a few weeks before. Sleepily, heavily, he tried to fix his mind upon it and recall it. What was it that Doctor Snodgrass had said? Ah, yes. That it was a mistake to pause here in reading the verse. We must read on without a pause. *Lay not up treasures upon earth where moth and rust do corrupt and where thieves break through and steal*—that was the true doctrine. Our treasures upon earth must not be put into unsafe places but into safe places. A most comforting doctrine! He had always followed it. Moths and rust and thieves had done no harm to his investments.

John Weightman's drooping eyes turned to the next verse, at the top of the second column.

"But lay up for yourselves treasures in heaven."

Now what had the Doctor said about that? How was it to be understood—in what sense, treasures—in heaven?

The book seemed to float away from him. The light vanished. He sank slowly forward upon the table. His head rested upon his folded hands. He slipped into the unknown.

* * *

How long afterward conscious life returned to him he did not know. The blank might have been an hour, or a century. He knew only that something had happened in the interval. What it was he could not tell. He found great difficulty in catching the thread of his identity again. He felt that he was himself, but the trouble was to make his connections, to verify and place himself, to know who and where he was.

At last it grew clear. John Weightman was sitting on a stone, a little way off from a road, in a strange country. The road was not a formal highway, fenced and graded. It was more like a great travel trace, worn by thousands of feet passing across the open country in the same direction. Down in the valley into which he could look, the road seemed to form itself gradually out of many minor paths, little footways coming across the meadows, winding tracks following along beside the streams, faintly marked trails emerging from the woodlands. But on the hillside the threads were more firmly woven into one clear band of travel, though there were still a few dim paths joining it here and there, as if persons had been climbing up the hill by other ways and had turned at last to seek the road.

From the edge of the hill, where John Weightman sat, he could see the travelers, in little groups or larger companies, gathering from time to time by the different paths and making the ascent. They were all clothed in white, and the form of their garments was strange to him; it was like some old picture. They passed him, group after group, talking quietly together or singing, not moving in haste but with a certain air of eagerness and joy, as if they were glad to be on their way to an appointed place. They did not stay to speak to him, but they looked at him often and spoke to one another as they looked; and now and then one of them would smile and beckon him a friendly greeting, so that he felt they would like him to be with them.

There was quite an interval between the groups sometimes, and he followed each of them with his eyes after it had passed, blanching the long ribbon of the road for a little transient space, rising and receding across the wide, billowy upland, among the rounded hillocks of aerial green and gold and lilac, until it came to the high horizon and stood outlined for a moment, a tiny cloud of whiteness against the tender blue before it vanished over the hill.

For a long time he sat there watching and wondering. It was a very different world from that in which his mansion on the Avenue was built; and it looked strange to him, but most real—as real as anything he had ever seen. Presently he felt a strong desire to know what country it was and where the people were going. He had a faint premonition of what it must be, but he wished to be sure. So he rose from the stone where he was sitting

and came down through the short grass and the lavender flowers toward a passing group of people. One of them turned to meet him and held out his hand. It was an old man, under whose white beard and brows John Weightman thought he saw a suggestion of the face of the village doctor who had cared for him years ago, when he was a boy in the country.

"Welcome!" said the old man. "Will you come with us?"

"Where are you going?"

"To the heavenly city to see our mansions there."

"And who are these with you?"

"Strangers to me until a little while ago; I know them better now. But you I have known for a long time, John Weightman. Don't you remember your old doctor?"

"Yes!" he cried. "Yes! Your voice has not changed at all. I'm glad indeed to see you, Doctor McLean, especially now. All this seems very strange to me, almost oppressive. I wonder if— But may I go with you, do you suppose?"

"Surely," answered the doctor, with his familiar smile. "It will do you good. And you also must have a mansion in the city waiting for you—a fine one, too. Are you not looking forward to it?"

"Yes," replied the other, hesitating a moment. "Yes, I believe it must be so, although I had not expected to see it so soon. But I will go with you, and we can talk along the way."

The two men quickly caught up with the other people, and all went forward together along the road. The doctor had little to tell of his experience, for it had been a plain, hard life, uneventfully spent for others, and the story of the village was very simple. John Weightman's adventures and triumphs would have made a far richer, more imposing history, full of contacts with the great events and personages of the time. But, somehow or other, he did not care to speak much about it, walking on that wide heavenly moorland under that tranquil, sunless arch of blue, in that free air of perfect peace, where the light was diffused without a shadow, as if the spirit of life in all things were luminous.

There was only one person besides the doctor in that little company whom John Weightman had known before—an old bookkeeper who had spent his life over a desk, carefully keeping accounts; a rusty, dull little man, patient and narrow, whose wife had been in the insane asylum for 20 years, and whose only child was a crippled daughter, for whose comfort and happiness he had toiled and sacrificed himself without stint. It was a surprise to find him here, as carefree and joyful as the rest.

The lives of the others in the company were revealed in brief glimpses as they talked together: a mother, early widowed, who had kept her little flock of children together and labored through hard and heavy years to bring them up in purity and knowledge. A Sister of Charity, who had devoted herself to the nursing of poor folk who were being eaten to death by cancer. A schoolmaster, whose heart and life had been poured into his quiet work of training boys for a clean and thoughtful manhood. A medical missionary, who had given up a brilliant career in science to take the charge of a hospital in darkest Africa. A beautiful woman with silver hair, who had resigned her dreams of love and marriage to care for an invalid father, and after his death had made her

life a long, steady search for ways of doing kindnesses to others. A poet, who had walked among the crowded tenements of a great city, bringing cheer and comfort not only by his lyrics, but by his wise and patient works for the downtrodden. A paralyzed woman who had lain for 30 years upon her bed, helpless but not hopeless, succeeding by a miracle of courage in her single aim: never to complain but always to impart a bit of her joy and peace to everyone who came near her. All these, and other persons like them, people of little consideration in the world, but now seemingly all full of great contentment and an inward gladness that made their steps light, were in the company that passed along the road, talking together of things past and things to come, and singing now and then with clear voices from which the veil of age and sorrow was lifted.

John Weightman joined in some of the songs that were familiar to him from their use in the church, at first with a touch of hesitation, and then more confidently. For as they went on, his sense of strangeness and fear at his new experience diminished, and his thoughts began to take on their habitual assurance and complacency. Were not these people going to the Celestial City? And was not he in his rightful place among them? He had always looked forward to this journey. If they were sure, each one, of finding a mansion there, could not he be far more sure? His life had been more fruitful than theirs. He had been a leader, a founder of new enterprises, a pillar of church and state, a prince of the house of Israel. Ten talents had been given him, and he had made them 20. His reward would be proportionate. He was glad that his companions were going to find fit dwellings prepared for them, but he thought also with a certain pleasure of the surprise that some of them would feel when they saw his appointed mansion.

So they came to the summit of the moorland and looked over into the world beyond. It was a vast green plain, softly rounded like a shallow vase and circled with hills of amethyst. A broad shining river flowed through it, and many silver threads of water were woven across the green; and there were borders of tall trees on the banks of the river, and orchards full of roses abloom along the little streams, and in the midst of it all stood the city, white and wonderful and radiant.

When the travelers saw it they were filled with awe and joy. They passed over the little streams and among the orchards quickly and silently, as if they feared to speak lest the city should vanish.

The wall of the city was very low (a child could see over it), for it was made only of precious stones, which are never large. The gate of the city was not like a gate at all, for it was not barred with iron or wood but only a single pearl, softly gleaming, marking the place where the wall ended and the entrance lay open.

A person stood there whose face was bright and grave, and whose robe was like the flower of the lily; not a woven fabric but a living texture. "Come in," he said to the company of travelers, "you are at your journey's end, and your mansions are ready for you."

John Weightman hesitated, for he was troubled by a doubt. Suppose that he was not really like his companions at his journey's end, but only transported for a little while out of the regular course of his life into this mysterious experience. Suppose that, as he dimly felt, he had not really passed through the door of death like these others, but only through the door of dreams and was walking in a vision, a living man among the blessed dead. Would it be right for him to go with them into the heavenly city? Would it not be a deception, a desecration, a deep and unforgivable offense? The strange, confusing question had no reason in it, as he very well knew; for if he was dreaming, then it was all a dream. But if his companions were real, then he also was with them in reality. Yet he could not rid his mind of the sense that there was a difference between them and him, and it made him afraid to go on. But as he paused and turned, the keeper of the gate looked straight and deep into his eyes and beckoned to him. Then he knew that it was not only right but necessary that he should enter.

They passed from street to street among fair and spacious dwellings, set in amaranthine gardens and adorned with an infinitely varied beauty of divine simplicity. The mansions differed in size, in shape, in charm: each one seemed to have its own personal look of loveliness, yet all were alike in fitness to their place, in harmony with one another, in the addition which each made to the singular and tranquil splendor of the city.

As the little company came, one by one, to the mansions which were prepared for them, and their guide beckoned to the happy inhabitant to enter in and take possession, there was a soft murmur of joy, half wonder and half recognition, as if the new and immortal dwelling were crowned with the beauty of surprise, lovelier and nobler than all the dreams of it had been; and yet also as if it were touched with the beauty of the familiar, the remembered, the long-loved. One after another the travelers were led to their own mansions, and went in gladly; and from within, through the open doorways, came sweet voices of welcome, and low laughter, and song.

At last there was no one left with the guide but the two old friends, Doctor McLean and John Weightman. They were standing in front of one of the largest and fairest of the houses, whose garden glowed softly with radiant flowers. The guide laid his hand upon the doctor's shoulder.

"This is for you," he said. "Go in; there is no more pain here, no more death, nor sorrow, nor tears; for your old enemies are all conquered. But all the good you have done for others, all the help you have given, all the comfort you have brought, all the strength and love you have bestowed, are here; for we have built them all into this mansion for you."

The good man's face was lightened with a still joy. He clasped his old friend's hand closely, and whispered, "How wonderful it is! Go on; you will come to your mansion next. It is not far away, and we shall see each other again soon, very soon."

So he went through the garden and into the music within. The keeper of the gate turned to John Weightman with level, quiet, searching eyes. Then he asked gravely, "Where do you wish me to lead you now?"

"To see my own mansion," answered the man with half-concealed excitement. "Is there not one here for me? You may not let me enter it yet, perhaps, for I must confess to you that I am only—"

"I know," said the keeper of the gate, "I know it all. You are John Weightman."

"Yes," said the man, more firmly than he had spo-

ken at first, for it gratified him that his name was known. "Yes, I am John Weightman, Senior Warden of St. Petronius' Church. I wish very much to see my mansion here, if only for a moment. I believe that you have one for me. Will you take me to it?"

The keeper of the gate drew a little book from the breast of his robe and turned over the pages. "Certainly," he said, with a curious look at the man, "your name is here; and you shall see your mansion, if you will follow me."

It seemed as if they must have walked miles and miles through the vast city, passing street after street of houses larger and smaller, of gardens richer and poorer, but all full of beauty and delight. They came into a kind of suburb, where there were many small cottages with plots of flowers, very lowly but bright and fragrant. Finally they reached an open field, bare and lonely-looking. There were two or three little bushes in it, without flowers, and the grass was sparse and thin. In the center of the field was a tiny hut, hardly big enough for a shepherd's shelter. It looked as if it had been built of discarded things, scraps and fragments of other buildings, put together with care and pains by someone who had tried to make the most of cast-off material. There was something pitiful and shamefaced about the hut. It shrank and drooped and faded in its barren field and seemed to cling only by sufferance to the edge of the splendid city.

"This," said the keeper of the gate, standing still and speaking with a low, distinct voice, "this is your mansion, John Weightman."

An almost intolerable shock of grieved wonder and

indignation choked the man for a moment so that he could not say a word. Then he turned his face away from the poor little hut and began to remonstrate eagerly with his companion.

"Surely, sir," he stammered, "you must be in error about this. There is something wrong—some other John Weightman—a confusion of names—the book must be mistaken."

"There is no mistake," said the keeper of the gate very calmly. "Here is your name, the record of your title and your possessions in this place."

"But how could such a house be prepared for me," cried the man, with a resentful tremor in his voice, "for me, after my long and faithful service? Is this a suitable mansion for one so well known and devoted? Why is it so pitifully small and mean? Why have you not built it large and fair, like the others?"

"That is all the material you sent us."

"What!"

"We have used all the material that you sent us," repeated the keeper of the gate.

"Now I know that you are mistaken," cried the man, with growing earnestness, "for all my life long I have been doing things that must have supplied you with material. Have you not heard that I have built a schoolhouse, the wing of a hospital, two—yes, three—small churches, and the greater part of a large one, the spire of Saint Petro—"

The keeper of the gate lifted his hand. "Wait," he said. "We know all these buildings. They were not ill done. But they were all marked and used as foundations for the name and mansion of John Weightman in the world. Did you not plan them for that?"

"Yes," answered the man, confused and taken aback. "I confess that I thought often of them in that way. Perhaps my heart was set upon that too much. But there are other things—my endowment for the college, my steady and liberal contributions to all the established charities, my support of every respectable—"

"Wait," said the keeper of the gate again. "Were not all these carefully recorded on earth where they would add to your credit? They were not foolishly done. Verily, you have had your reward for them. Would you be paid twice?"

"No!" cried the man, with deepening dismay. "I dare not claim that. I acknowledge that I considered my own interest too much. But surely not altogether! You have said that these things were not foolishly done. They accomplished some good in the world. Does not that count for something?"

"Yes," answered the keeper of the gate, "it counts in the world, where you counted it. But it does not belong to you here. We have saved and used everything that you sent us. This is the mansion prepared for you."

As he spoke his look grew deeper and more searching, like a flame of fire. John Weightman could not endure it. It seemed to strip him naked and wither him. He sank to the ground under the crushing weight of shame, covering his eyes with his hands, and cowering face downward upon the stones. Dimly through the trouble of his mind he felt their hardness and coldness.

"Tell me, then," he cried, brokenly, "since my life has been of so little worth, how came I here at all?"

"Through the mercy of the King." The answer was

like the soft tolling of a bell.

"And how have I earned it?" he murmured.

"It is never earned; it is only given," came the clear, low reply.

"But how have I failed so wretchedly," he asked, "in all the purpose of my life? What could I have done better? What is it that counts here?"

"Only that which is truly given," answered the bell-like voice. "Only that good which is done for the love of doing it. Only those plans in which the welfare of others is the master thought. Only those labors in which the sacrifice is greater than the wages. Only those gifts in which the giver forgets himself."

The man lay silent. A great weakness, an unspeakable despondency and humiliation, were upon him. But the face of the keeper of the gate was infinitely tender as he bent over him.

"Think again, John Weightman. Has there been nothing like that in your life?"

"Nothing," he sighed. "If there ever were such things it must have been long ago. They were all crowded out—I have forgotten them."

There was an ineffable smile on the face of the keeper of the gate, and his hand made the sign of the cross over the bowed head as he spoke gently. "These are the things that the King never forgets, and because there were a few of them you have a little place here."

The sense of coldness and hardness under John Weightman's hands grew sharper and more distinct. The feeling of bodily weariness and lassitude weighed upon him, but there was a calm, almost a lightness, in his heart as he listened to the fading vibrations of the silvery bell-tones. The chimney clock on the mantel had just ended the last stroke of 7:00 as he lifted his head from the table. Thin, pale strips of the city morning were falling into the room through the narrow partings of the heavy curtains.

What was it that had happened to him? Had he been ill? Had he fainted away? Or had he only slept, and had his soul gone visiting in dreams? He sat for some time, motionless, not lost but finding himself in thought. Then he took a narrow book from the table drawer, wrote a check, and tore it out.

He went slowly up the stairs, knocked very softly at his son's door, and, hearing no answer, entered without noise. Harold was asleep, his bare arms thrown above his head, and his eager face relaxed in peace. His father looked at him a moment with strangely shining eyes, and then tiptoed quietly to the writing desk, found a pencil and a sheet of paper, and wrote rapidly:

"My dear boy, here is what you asked me for. Do what you like with it, and ask for more if you need it. If you are still thinking of that work with Grenfell, we'll talk it over today after church. I want to know your heart better, and if I have made mistakes—"

A slight noise made him turn his head. Harold was sitting up in bed with wide-open eyes.

"Father!" he cried, "is that you?"

"Yes, my son," answered John Weightman; "I've come back—I mean, I've come up—No; I mean come in— Well, here I am, and God give us a good Christmas together."

---

* Billions, in today's money.

Full Circle

Lloyd Decker

*Here he was alone in a foreign country at Christmas.
Alone and destitute, for apparently a pickpocket had relieved
him of his wallet. And he had no one to vouch for him.*
Or so he thought.

My father had a saying that precisely described my feelings. When someone had gotten the best of him in a business venture or he had done something of which he was not particularly proud, he would shake his head and say, "I feel as if I were seven kinds of fool!"

And that is exactly the way I felt at that moment—as if I were seven kinds of fool.

After a lifetime of travel as a member of the U. S. Army and almost continuous travel since retiring from the service, it had finally happened to me. Upon my arrival at the main railroad station in Frankfurt, Germany, the previous evening, I discovered that my wallet was missing. It had contained my credit cards, a ticket good for a return flight to New York and all of my available cash, with the exception of a few German marks obtained in Parks and carried loosely in a trouser pocket. A folder of traveler's checks, which I had placed in a coat pocket, was also gone.

Thoroughly disgusted, I just couldn't believe that I'd somehow managed to lose it all. There had been a certain amount of the usual jostling through the crowd and struggling with baggage while boarding the train at the station in Paris. Perhaps the gentleman who apologized profusely after almost knocking me down had had a light-fingered partner in the charming young lady who "graciously" saved me from a fall.

This was not my first trip to Germany and I was not completely unfamiliar with Frankfurt. I had passed through the city during World War II and had been stationed there for a time during the early 1950s after a tour in Eschwege. So, upon discovering that I had suddenly become a pauper, I carried my suitcase to a small hotel (remembered for its superb location and excellent *weinstube*) located on a narrow lane of the *Gatleut Strasse*.

It was a rather crisp evening and snow crunched under foot as I hurried along. Christmas tree lights glistened through frost-patterned windows and the notes of a carol dropped into the thin air from speakers mounted atop old wrought-iron lamp posts. Tomorrow would be Christmas Eve.

Despite an absence of 20 years, I had no difficulty finding my way. Upon arrival at my hotel, I was relieved to learn that they were holding my request for a reservation. I felt guilty about checking in with empty pockets and imagined that the desk clerk hesitated and regarded me rather suspiciously. I desperately hoped he would not ask for a credit card or a cash deposit and was relieved when he did not.

My room was spacious, brightly clean, and filled with well-polished furniture. A few ornaments and bits of tinsel were scattered about the room, and a tiny artificial Christmas tree was centered on the mantelpiece.

The desk downstairs had a message for me. Friends traveling elsewhere in Europe who were to have met me in Frankfurt to share Christmas had a sudden change of plans. They couldn't make it.

Some Christmas! I was alone and broke in a foreign city. I promptly sent my stateside bank a telegram requesting the immediate transfer of funds to a German bank not far from my hotel. Then I dined alone on the only thing I could afford: sausages and rolls at one of those sidewalk stands so common in German cities.

I left the hotel late the following morning, feeling that it would give the bank time to respond to my telegram. I would walk and save the few remaining marks I possessed. While strolling across a corner of the plaza in front of the railroad station, my eyes shifted to a spot where I had seen a dead German soldier lying my first time in Frankfurt during the war. He had looked like everyone's younger brother, about 15, small and twisted; his face wore a look of sad surprise and he was clad in a uniform much too large for his immature frame, like a boy who had been playing soldier. It was one of those things that a soldier finds difficult to forget.

* * *

This entire trip had been planned as something of a sentimental journey, a retracing of steps. As I entered the *Kaiser Strasse* and walked through crowds of prosperous shoppers, my mind dwelled on thoughts of a previous Christmas in Germany. It had been during that grim winter of 1948, before the fruition of the Marshal Plan and the German recovery, before the cities rose above the rubble once again. Those were days of hunger and despair for the Germans.

The contrast between then and now was remarkable. I had turned into *Taunus Anlage Strasse* and shortly thereafter stood before a teller in an imposing (and intimidating) bank that boasted branches throughout the world.

I introduced myself and stated my business. The bank teller was patient and courteous, but no, an authorization for funds in my name had not been received.

Would he please check once again?

"Of course, but the answer must still be the same, sir."

I felt a bit desperate. This bank would be closing for a long bank holiday in less than one hour. Because of the time differential, my bank in the United States was already closed. The authorization was almost certainly en route.

When I explained these circumstances to the bank teller and cautiously suggested a temporary loan, he simultaneously raised his eyebrows and hands and exclaimed, "But sir, I am sure you will understand! We don't even know you and certainly have no way of knowing if these monies will ever arrive!" Then he smiled and added, "I am very sorry." That apparently was intended to be the end of our discussion.

I stared at the tinsel and the miniature Santas and the silver bells decorating the ornate grillwork of the teller's cage and felt as if I were seven kinds of fool. Twenty-seven years in the Army had made me tolerant of others but very impatient with the kind of situation I'd permitted myself to blunder into. Then as I turned to go, a voice called through the open door of an office located behind the teller:

"Will you please wait one moment, sir? *Herr* Engler, come here, please."

The teller excused himself and entered the office while members of the bank staff and customers nearby examined me with open curiosity. The teller returned very quickly and, bustling with goodwill and purpose, proclaimed: "We need not wait for a reply from your bank, sir. We can advance sufficient funds immediately on a note over your signature."

* * *

While I stood before him puzzling over this sudden turn of events, *Herr* Engler quickly filled out a brief form which he asked me to sign. Then he counted out a small stack of marks and handed it to me with a hearty, "There you are, sir, and Merry Christmas."

After thanking him and wishing him the same, I simply had to satisfy my growing curiosity.

"*Herr* Engler," I asked, "I don't understand. Please tell me what changed your mind about the loan. The note requires a cosigner. I can't provide one. I don't know anyone in Frankfurt."

Smiling broadly, eyes twinkling

with his secret, *Herr* Engler replied, "In this bank, sir, you have the best credentials and the best cosigner in all of Frankfurt."

* * *

As he spoke, a tall man strode from the rear office, rounded the partition and stopped a few feet from me. Grinning with delight and apparently hugely pleased with himself, the stranger asked, "Do you remember me, *Herr* Sergeant? It's Gunter!" He almost bounced as he vigorously emphasized each word.

Of course I remembered Gunter. I only found it difficult to absorb the fact that the tall young man who had so suddenly appeared before me was Gunter Mayer. His appearance had changed little through the years, except that stature and features of the man had overpowered those of the boy.

I had met his family by chance that terrible winter of 1948-49, in Eschwege, when Gunter was a gangling youth of 13. His father had been invalided from the Russian Front and had not fully recovered. Gunter's mother was desperately trying to hold the family together. They had nothing. Potatoes, and a limited supply of those, were their customary meal.

I had helped out with the contents of packages received from home and my mother had sent a special Christmas package that year. It wasn't any big deal—other Americans were doing the same—but I had felt fortunate to be able to help someone whose need was so great.

Frau Mayer had proved adept with needle and thread and altered an *"Ike"* jacket for me. Word spread, and she soon had a small sewing business going among the occupation forces.

When Gunter was satisfied that I really *did* recognize him, we shook hands, thumped each other's shoulders, and then shook hands once again. We were too excited to sit down as we traded information to fill a gap of two decades. Yes, his mother was well and his father had recovered his health and was now an official of the Federal Republic of Germany. Gunter was married, had two children, and was the manager of this bank.

No excuses, I must spend Christmas with them. When I protested that it was too much of an imposition, Gunter replied, *"Ach, Herr* Sergeant, I would not think of going home without you! We have never forgotten you or your kindness.

"My mother and father speak of you often and no Christmas in our home is complete without retelling the story of the American sergeant who gave us Christmas and helped us through our worst time. It is a family tradition! The children ask for the story. How *Wunderbar* to see you now!"

It was a memorable Christmas—hours of happy conversation in the warmth of the Mayer family's comfortable home, children searching for presents under a brightly lighted tree, crackling goose and venison, candlelight, wine, and carols.

What had seemed to have begun as a thoroughly miserable holiday season in a cold, foreign land had turned out to be one of the most pleasant I have ever spent. My life had indeed come full circle: an almost forgotten event—a simple, charitable act—was unexpectedly reciprocated during a time of need a full 20 years later.

Even When Nobody's Home

Joseph Leininger Wheeler

Why should they spend so much money to fly back to see his mother when she wouldn't even recognize them if they did go?

Why indeed?

"Claire, do you think we ought to fly back and see her?"

"Well, you tell me, John. She's *your* mother!"

"I know she's my mother. . . . It's just that—it's just—"

"It's just that she'll probably not even know we're there—is that what you're trying to say?"

"Well, yes. And, uh—"

"And with our finances being pretty tight right now, you're wondering if we ought to spend all that money without assurances."

"But Claire, you know there can be no assurances that she'll know us."

"Let me get this straight: just what is it that you're trying to say about your mother and about us? Let's get it out into the open. If, when we next see her and look into her eyes, there's no awareness (for there's never anyone home any more), then that means our trip money was spent foolishly? If, on the other hand, she actually recognizes us, knows we're there then it will have been a wise investment? Is that what you're trying to say?"

"Putting it that way, it does sound crass and self-serving, doesn't it? Sounds as if we care more for ourselves than for her."

"Well, doesn't it, John? Your mother gave birth to you, raised you to be a son she could be proud of, yet somehow it appears that you begrudge the cost of two plane tickets and the expenses for lodging and food. Besides, what signal do you think this sends to the kids?"

"Oh, come now, Claire, they can't hear us talk. They're a long way—"

"Don't be dense! All three of them keep mighty close tabs on us. They know how long it's been since we've flown back to see her. They also know we've found time and money to take a cruise during that time. It isn't merely that they know how long it has been, did you ever think about one of life's most certain probabilities? Our children will treat us the same way we treat our parents."

Silence. A *long* silence.

The Flight West

"Just trying to remember whether or not I locked all the windows before we left."

"We did, John; I double-checked."

"Good. Couldn't help worrying, we left home in such a rush."

John returns to his book, and Claire looks out the

window again, to the snow-capped peaks far below. Sometime later she looks away and sees him staring off into space, paying no attention to the book on his lap. Smiling, she says, "A penny for your thoughts, dear."

"Oh, I've just been thinking—been thinking a lot."

"About what?"

"About us . . . About Mom . . . Our kids . . . Life . . . Priorities. Oh, yes; and about Dad."

"And?"

"Well, do you remember the poem I wrote just before Dad died?"

"You mean 'October Snow,' the one you wrote on the plane, flying back from visiting your father?"

"Yes. In a very real sense there's a seamless connection between it and this sudden Christmas trip. I can't get the words out of my head."

"Refresh my memory, dear. I do know I was greatly moved by it. Do you think you can still remember the words?"

"Certainly. Give me a minute. . . . Here goes"

"The snow falls once again;
Oh, granted it fell last October
So much the same way
The lens of my camera
Might reveal little difference.
But I know the difference:
The sand of another year
Has dropped with deadly certainty
From the future into the past.

My life force is one year less
Than it was last October—

Another scene in the drama of my life,
Another curtain fall;
Another song from my libretto now sung;
Another corner of the canvas now painted in—
And the leaves have begun to fall.

Gold to green to gold,
And then white once again;
Spring to summer to autumn,
And then winter once again;
Morning to noon to evening,
And then night once again.

Snow is an ending,
A terminal mark of punctuation;
The world will not be the same
Next autumn when it falls again:
Many an insect, many a bird, many an animal—
Many a friend
Will not see the snow of next October;
Who knows? Maybe not even I
Will be there to see it fall.

But sufficient unto the day is the freight thereof;
It is enough to know that snow is falling again,
That the child in me rushes out to greet it—
Revels in it, sings in it, cries in it, laughs in it,
Is renewed in it.

For . . . if the snow brings an end to summer . . .
It also makes possible another spring.

© 1996

After a poignant period of silence, during which neither is capable of speech, Claire says, "And you strongly suspected when you wrote that, didn't you, that you might never see Dad alive again?"

"Yes."

"And now?"

"Well, now, it's Mom. And with her it's actually worse than it was with Dad, for after the one love of her life left her, she quickly left us. Oh, I know doctors have medical terms for it—words such as 'ministrokes' and 'dementia'—but you and I both know that's all medical gobbledygook! That's not why she went downhill so fast."

"Broken heart?"

"Without question. Without him, she just could not face days and nights empty of his presence, so her mind slammed the door on the real world. Of course she's still with us, physically, but only as a shell of her former self. What's left of that wondrous singing spirit is imprisoned behind those shuttered eyes. When I think of my mother, it's not that silent thing that resides in a little box of a room in Oregon but rather what she *was*—that young woman so vibrantly alive with love for God, for Dad, for her children. Her near photographic memory, able to remember, word-for-word, thousands of short stories, readings, and poems (even complete books such as Longfellow's *Hiawatha* and *Evangeline*); complete menus of every dish served on Thanksgivings

and Christmases through the years—even half a century before! Oh, yes! And how could I forget that memorable day when, in the back seat of our car, one of Mom's sisters asked her about the church service she'd missed!"

"Oh, John, that was *rich*! Wasn't her answer all about clothes?"

"It was indeed—a person-by-person account of what each member of the congregation was wearing, including such things as colors, hairdos, and shoes. Oh, my! Now I'm wondering whether she was listening to Dad's sermons at all those years!"

"I'm curious, John. What was it like living with her when you were young?"

"Well, if anyone ever was in love with life—with every breath, every nuance of it—it was she! Perish the thought if one of her children was not learning and growing every minute of the day. On trips she always brought along a big stack of interesting articles and stories to read to us. For Mom, the day was never long enough for all she wanted to do and learn. And if I were to encapsulate her entire life by one poem I could not possibly improve on the poem she always ended the 'Cradle to the Golden Gate' programs she and Dad put on late in life."

"You mean, of course, 'A Song of Living.' I've come to love that poem so much I memorized it myself."

"Good. It's your turn, then, to recite a poem to *me*."

"Gladly."

"A Song of Living"
Because I have loved life, I shall have no sorrow to die.
I have sent up my gladness on wings to be lost in the blue of the sky;

I have run and leaped with the rain, I have taken the wind to my breast.
My cheek like a drowsy child to the face of the earth I have pressed.
Because I have loved life, I shall have no sorrow to die.

I have kissed young love on the lips; I have heard his song to the end.
I have struck my hand like a seal in the loyal hand of a friend;
I have known the peace of heaven, the comfort of work done well.
I have longed for death in the darkness and risen alive out of hell.
Because I have loved life, I have no sorrow to die.

I give a share of my soul to the world where my course is run.
I know that another shall finish the task that I leave undone.
I know that no flower, no flint, was in vain on the path I trod.
As one looks on a face through a window, through life, I have looked on God.
Because I have loved life, I shall have no sorrow to die.

–Amelia Burr

"Bravo, Claire! And that last line will most certainly hold true for Mom."

"How true . . . And we mustn't forget her voluminous correspondence, John. In a way, it was her way of

124

ministering to others, of making a difference."

"And she was not only blessed with poems, readings, stories, menus, and clothes, she was equally blessed with *people*. She was absolutely fascinated by men, women, and children, what made each one unique. I remember how she was always putting the touch on people, in person and by mail, helping children gain an education."

"It must have been amazing to have been home-schooled by her."

"Oh, it was! Fourteen of the first 16 years of my life were spent in her presence. She set my sails and filled me with a love for literature and beautiful things. Encouraged me to devour a big stack of books each week. Encouraged me to dream."

"How different that serene world, John, from the frenzied pace of childhood today."

"Didn't realize how lucky I was."

"You know, dear, I hadn't known just how much of a romantic your father really was until we unearthed all those Valentine's Day cards in that old trunk. What passion in those inked-in passages! Almost felt we were intruding into a world not meant for us. Your mother obviously cherished them for she kept every last one."

"You're right. Guess we kids just took that enduring romance for granted. Assumed everyone's parents loved each other the way they did. That gave us *such* a secure feeling, knowing their love for each other was the very bedrock of our existence."

Was the Trip Worth It?

"Mom looked good, didn't she? That outfit she had on really became her. . . . And weren't the Christmas decorations beautiful? So special for Callahan Court to make the place so festive for everyone."

"Claire, Claire; none of that makes up for Mom not recognizing us. Once or twice, I'll admit, I thought I saw a glimmer of recognition, but the light of awareness never came on."

"It was still worthwhile, John. The entire staff notices when family members care enough about someone to come see them. Just imagine how terrible it would be if no one loved her enough to come!"

"Some members of our family apparently feel that since Mom's no longer the vivacious person she once was, far better to stay away completely. Perhaps it makes them feel uncomfortable—even vulnerable themselves—to see her so. . . . Yet, lest we feel too self-righteous, we've been close to making the same mistake, Claire, so we better not be too judgmental about them."

"I beg your pardon!" Clare gives him an icy stare. "What's this 'we' business? *Who* should be feeling self-righteous?"

"Stop! Stop! I get the message. It's *I*—never you."

"You're forgiven. At least she seems happy. In fact, Freda told me that all her employees love your mom. She always has a smile for everyone."

"Well, I guess we can be happy for *that*. . . . So what do we do with tomorrow, all the time we have left?"

"More of the same, I guess. She didn't even look twice at the Christmas presents we brought her—just let them drop to the floor and dozed off again. She sleeps so much of the time these days."

"Claire, I'd like to try an experiment with Mom tomorrow. It can't hurt, and who knows? Maybe we'll get a flash of awareness out of her."

"So what's your suggestion? I'm game to try almost anything—goodness knows nothing else works."

"Well, it just came to me today that since Mom has always loved the Christmas season so much, and since, in her many stage performances, she often recited by memory her favorite Christmas stories, I thought it might be interesting to read one of her favorites out loud and see what her reaction might be."

"Let's do it! Which one?"

"Christine Whiting Parmenter's ultimate tear-jerker, 'David's Star of Bethlehem.' Mom never could get to the end of it without coming close to breaking down."

"If *any* story can break through that glazed look in her eyes, it would have to be that one."

"David's Star of Bethlehem"

The next day, John takes out a collection of Christmas stories and tells his mother that he's going to read her one of them. She pays no attention to him at all, even after he begins reading. The same holds true as he reads about how Scott and Nancy Carson flee their home town because they can't handle the holiday-related memories associated with the death of their only child, Jimmy, three years ago this Christmas day. So they take a train into the mountains where no one will remind them that it's Christmas.

It is as the Carsons approach their remote cabin in the snow that Claire first notices the tiniest tensing in the unresponsive woman so close yet so far from her:

"They stopped simultaneously as a clear, sweet voice sounded from within the cabin:

"'Silent night, holy night . . . '

"Scott's face went suddenly dead white. He threw out a hand as if to brush something away, but Nancy caught it in hers, pulling it close against her wildly beating heart.

"'All is calm . . . all is bright. '

"The childish treble came weirdly from within, while Nancy cried, 'Scott, dearest, don't let go! It's only the little boy singing the carols he's learned in school. Don't you see? Come! Pull yourself together. We must go in.'"

As John reads and turns the pages, his mother continues to stare at him, but without any indication that, deep within, anything is registering.

Some time later, as he nears the end of the long story, Claire can tell by her husband's body language and inflections that he's resigned to chalking up this experiment as a failure, too, but he gamely plows ahead:

"'He drew the boy onto his knees and went on quietly, 'The stores were closed, David, when I reached the village. I couldn't buy you a Christmas gift, you see. But I thought if we gave you a *real* mother and—and a *father*.'"

Suddenly, another voice breaks in: "'Oh, Scott!'" it says, and Mother continues as though she'd been reciting from the story's very beginning:

"'It was a cry of rapture from Nancy. Seeing the child's bewilderment, she explained, 'He means, dear, that you're our boy now, for always.'"

Wordlessly, John takes Claire's hand.

Steadily, the reader continues, her voice gaining strength and power as she reaches that memorable conclusion:

"'It was David who spoke next. He was leaning close to the window, his elbows resting on the sill, his face cupped in his two hands. He seemed to have forgotten them as he said dreamily, 'It's Christmas. Silent night . . . holy night . . . like the song. I wonder'—he looked up trustingly into the faces above him—'I wonder if—if maybe one of them stars isn't the Star of Bethlehem!'"

Slowly, the reader turns to John and says, "You . . . always . . . *loved* . . . that . . . sto–ry!" Then the light of awareness flickers out in her eyes. Once again, no one is at home.

There is a long silence as John and Claire just look at each other, unable to fully digest what they have just experienced.

"Best Christmas present I ever got!" John says finally.

"Oh, John, what if we hadn't come!"

Epilogue

This true-to-life story completes my trilogy, "His Last Christmas" (the story of the last days of my father's life in *Christmas in My Heart 8*) and "Three C's for Comfort," from *Smoky, the Ugliest Cat in the World and Other Great Cat Stories* (the story of my mother's last days and the remarkable cat that comforts all who mourn in Callahan Court in Roseburg, Oregon). "David's Star of Bethlehem" may be found in *Christmas in My Heart 1*.

I wrote "October Snow" as I returned home from seeing my father alive for the last time in 1996. We were told by those who cherished my mother about a day when one of them started reading one of her favorite Christmas stories out loud. My usually unresponsive Mother stunned the reader by breaking in and reciting the text from memory herself before again fading out of reality. Although those afflicted by dementia lose the ability to converse naturally in the real world, if someone can just break through to a once-memorized story or poem, that verbal train of words may still be intact and can still run down the track of memory.

It has taken me 10 years to cycle through the grief associated with the passing of both of my parents. It is my prayerful wish that the thoughts and insights I share in these three stories will encourage and inspire others who are going through these same dark days with their own parents, spouses, or loved ones.

I close with eight lines from a century old poem that hangs in my office. It reflects the depth of my mother's love for my father better perhaps than anything I could ever write:

"The night has a thousand eyes,
*   And the day but one;*
Yet the light of the bright world dies
*   With the dying sun.*

The mind has a thousand eyes,
*   And the heart but one;*
Yet the light of a whole world dies
*   When love is done."*

– Francis William Bourdillon
(1852 - 1921)